At the Edge of a Dark Forest

CONNIE ALMONY

Copyright 2014 Connie Almony

Cover Design by Vanessa Riley

ISBN-13: 978-1495452178
ISBN-10: 1495452174

All rights reserved. No part of this publication may be reproduced in any form, stored in any retrieval system, posted on any website, or transmitted in any form or by any means, without permission from the publisher, except for brief quotations in printed reviews and articles.

Scripture taken from the HOLY BIBLE, NEW INTERNATIONAL VERSIONS ®. Copyright © 1973, 1978, 1984 by International Bible Society. Used by permission of Zondervan Publishing House. All rights reserved.

The "NIV" and "New International Versions" trademarks are registered in the United States Parent and Trademark Office by International Bible Society. Use of either trademark requires the permission of International Bible Society.

This novella is a work of fiction. Any mention of real events, businesses, organization and locales is intended only to give the fiction a sense of reality. Names of characters, incidents, and dialogues are solely the product of this author's imagination and are not expected to be considered real. Any resemblance to actual persons, living or dead, is entirely coincidental.

Author Note: The innovative frame design of the prosthetic socket mentioned in this story is a true product that is improving the lives of many amputees. See the Acknowledgements at the end of this novel for more information regarding the developer and the company that provides it.

Dedication

To all the men and women who have served in our armed forces, sacrificing much so we can remain free.

Greater love has no one than this, that he lay down his life for his friends. (John 15:13, NIV)

Table of Contents

Chapter One 7
Chapter Two 24
Chapter Three 34
Chapter Four 41
Chapter Five 51
Chapter Six 58
Chapter Seven 62
Chapter Eight 73
Chapter Nine 84
Chapter Ten 92
Chapter Eleven 102
Chapter Twelve 115
Chapter Thirteen 124
Chapter Fourteen 133
Chapter Fifteen 140
Chapter Sixteen 147
Chapter Seventeen 160
Chapter Eighteen 163
Author Note 172
Acknowledgements 173
Reading Group Questions 175
About the Author 178
More Fairwilde Reflections 179

Chapter One

Cole hobbled up the snow-covered path, his metal crutch doing the work of his missing left leg. He turned to climb the wooded hill to his favorite perch for one last look. Knowing it would take five times as long as it did when he was a kid—having two arms and two legs back then—he scrambled up the frozen incline, using his right arm stump and dragging the crutch along beside him. He'd been a Marine. He'd do this or die.

In fact, he was counting on the latter.

Cole could never take his own life. Somehow, the thought of his remaining manor staff finding his body didn't set well with him. Most of them had been on the payroll since before he was born and were more family than his own parents had been. No, he wouldn't leave his remains for them. But maybe he could challenge God—or at least the elements—enough to where one or the other would finally do the deed.

Was that what drove him to this climb during a blizzard in freezing temps? He'd told Mrs. Rivera, the housekeeper, he needed to go camping—a necessary means of transitioning from war to civilian life. Regardless of the fact he'd been transitioning for years now, and hadn't bothered to pack any gear.

She knew not to stop him. Not that she couldn't, given his current condition. But had she done that, it would have left him feeling more impotent than he did now. He suspected she knelt by her Baby Jesus statue, at this very moment, rolling beads through her fingers as she mouthed the Hail Mary over and over again.

Lotta good that would do.

Cole's moments "transitioning" only doubled in frequency rather than dwindled. He'd started back when he still wore a prosthetic arm and leg, but after months subjecting them to the cold and rain, night and day, they rubbed against his skin, chafing and burning, making him feel more caged than free. He'd finally chucked them over a precipice one morning, vowing never to wear any fake parts again.

He'd kept that vow. This was who he was. Not just after the IED, but before. Half a man. He'd always been half a man, scarred and disfigured. Only now his outsides displayed what his insides always suspected. No one knew that better than Beckett. And still Beckett had ...

He shook the thought from his mind as he scrambled higher to reach the perch that once made him feel king of the mountain. He could oversee his entire domain—the family's wooded acreage that rose and fell at angles as far as he could see. Now his. Solely his. No one left to share it with—except those he paid.

Today he didn't feel like a king. He made his way up the hill like a slithering beast, rustling through the powdery snow. The thump of the intact limb, then a pulling and dragging of the other through the slush. His body left a trail like a snake. That trail would soon be covered by the precipitation falling unceasingly on this night.

He reached the top and spied the mountain road that meandered far below. A snowplow's headlights traveled its length as it temporarily cleared the ice. No other lights followed. No one dared.

Cole collapsed into the plush snow, face to the emptying black sky. Snowflakes enlarged as they fell from the darkness into his eyes. Maybe his limbs—those left—would go numb before he froze to death. Would it be painful? He didn't know. He'd never experienced these kinds of elements in combat. He'd been more used to the heat—blistering heat. Heat so bad it made his vision blur, waves of air that crinkled ahead of him.

Boom!

He jolted at the vision of the IED bursting into flames. That had been real heat! In one instant Lance Corporal Beckett Forsythe had been beside him. The next—nothing but parts. And Cole had been left missing a few of his own.

Was that sweat dripping down his back in these frigid temps? More droplets formed icicles on his forehead. He struggled to slow his breaths, hoping his heartbeat would do the same. He lay back against the fluffy snow again. It wouldn't take long. The fingers on his left hand were already growing numb. He'd read somewhere people often hallucinated before hypothermia set in. Nothing new.

Crash!

Cole bolted up, wishing the visions weren't so real. But this didn't come with a vision. He looked around, fully aware of the frozen forest beneath his body and the vibration that had emanated with the sound.

He scrambled upright, pulled at his metal crutch, and rose to standing. Down the steep slope of the hill, a gouge in the guardrail opened to a trench through the snow. At the bottom lay a car mangled against a tree—its headlights a beacon to whomever might pass by.

No one would. Not on this night. Many roads had already been closed and only emergency vehicles and snow removal trucks traveled the others.

The only chance the driver had was Cole. Some chance. But Cole would not sit back and do nothing. He had to at least try to help. He couldn't let anyone else die just because he wanted to. Do or die trying. The latter still sounded best, but now he needed the former more.

He slid down the steep hill, using his crutch like a ski pole, guiding his trajectory toward the wreckage. Snow packed in under his jacket, melting into his skin. He shivered out the cold he had previously been inviting.

At the bottom he drove the crutch into the earth and pulled up. Under trees, the snow measured inches rather than feet. He could get to the disabled vehicle and check on the driver.

Flexing the fingers of his left hand, he worked out the numbness and cursed his luck. Why'd this jerk have to come out on *this* night, in *this* storm, on *this* mountain?

He trudged toward the car and peered inside. The driver blinked rapidly, his head swinging around as if coming out of a daze. He banged the deflated airbag at the wheel with his fist.

Cole pulled his wool cap lower against the scars running from his scalp into his face, and knocked on the window. The man jumped and turned, eyes white in their largeness.

"Let me help you."

The man seemed to take long moments to process the words then popped the latch on his door. It squealed and crunched. Cole yanked it open with his good hand against the folded metal at the hinge. It gave.

The man scanned Cole's length, no doubt assessing his missing limbs. His mouth dropped open. "You're ..." He slammed his fist against the steering wheel again and released a string of language Cole had only heard on the battlefield.

Yes. Cole was a beast. A slithering, angry beast. Uglier on the inside than on the out.

The man peered into the sky. "Lord! Must you continually remind me of my failings?"

Lord? Did this guy really think God would answer? "You comin' or not?"

The man's jaw jerked. He turned his white-cropped head away from Cole. "Not!"

Was Cole that ugly, that horrifying, the guy would rather die in the cold than trust Cole to bring him to safety?

"Look," Cole almost spit fire, "Your cell won't work up here and nobody'd come for you in this weather if it did." He nodded over his shoulder. "My house is just down a path over there. If we help each other out, we could both get there safely."

The man's brows drew together. Cole could almost feel the guy's gaze travel the length of him again, hovering at the stump below his right elbow and then the left thigh missing everything from what once had been a knee. Was that concern on his face? Cole steeled against the idiot's pity. He turned.

"Wait." The car door creaked as the man pushed it wider. "I'm coming with you."

~*~

Cole poured Irish Cream into his coffee as Mrs. Rivera scurried to prepare hot chocolate and cake for their guest. Henry, the man from the vehicle, sat wordlessly by the fire in the living room, wrapped in a blanket.

Mrs. Rivera eyed Cole's elixir. "You should lay off that poison," she said in her thick Mexican accent that hadn't lessened in the thirty years she'd lived in this country. "It'll keel you."

As if that would discourage him from using it. He took a long draw, the heat of the coffee thawing his body, the burn of the alcohol numbing his mind. He poured more coffee, then topped it off with Irish Cream. Mrs. Rivera tsked.

She rattled ahead of him, tray filled with goodies, to the living room where Henry waited. You'd think Henry was an angel sent by God the way she had attended to him, having made a fire, wrapping him in a blanket and taking out the best china for his impromptu visit to the Mansion.

She placed the tray on a coffee table in front of him and poured hot chocolate from the pitcher. He accepted the cup and glanced to Cole before dropping his gaze to the liquid inside. "Thank you."

"De nada." Did she just curtsey? "Let me know if you need anything else. I will prepare a room for you to stay the night."

Henry nodded and glanced at Cole in the archway between the rooms one more time. Did Henry fear him?

Mrs. Rivera took the coffee from Cole's hand. "Let me get this for you." She placed it on the table in front of Henry as if that were where Cole intended to sit. Hand free now, he grasped the metal crutch and hobbled over. Might as well not be a complete ogre to his uninvited guest—well, begrudgingly invited. Mrs. Rivera disappeared through the hall.

Henry turned to Cole and took him in, unflinchingly this time. His gaze traveled up the lonely leg, took in the right-arm stump, then hit on the scar from his upper lip that carved all the way up his left temple. Cole could almost feel the screech of brakes as the man's eyes halted—no doubt at the ugly etching pooled at the end of the scar on his purposely bald head. "How'd you lose your limbs?" This guy got right to the point.

"Iraq. IED."

Henry drew in a breath. "My younger brother lost his in Nam."

Cole wondered what sort of device did the job, but decided not to ask. "Arm and a leg?"

"Both legs."

"Oh."

Did Henry think they were kindred spirits now? Not! "How old is he?"

"He committed suicide on the five-year anniversary of his return." His brows drew together with a sense of anger and irony. What was he thinking? "I vowed to help others like him." His words were strained. "So they wouldn't feel …"

Cole waited for the rest of his sentence, but it didn't come. In fact, he didn't need it. His own bitterness churned against the lowering censors from the excess alcohol in his coffee. He glared at the man on his chair. "How does one help others like your brother?" His sarcasm grew as did the curl of his lip. "House him. Pamper him. Find jobs he can't do with people willing to make it easier for the crippled guy?"

Henry jolted. Tears hung on the edges of his eyes. "My company developed prosthetic limbs for amputees. At one time, it was the leader in research and development, giving the wounded lives closer to what they'd been before the loss."

Cole sensed more. "And now?"

"I gave control to my two sons when I retired early. They believed it wiser to cut costs than to build lives. They ran the company into the ground, peddling defective products that did more harm than good. They even gave bonuses to prosthetists who pushed inferior products."

Henry shifted, placed his mug on the table, his gaze never rising from it.

"Several months ago, a young veteran died when a seriously defective screw caused him to fall down a steep concrete stairway. Since the news coverage, other complaints have come in which have begun to lead to mass recalls."

Cole's breathing slowed as he took in the guilt that poured from this man's features, his posture, his mind.

Henry stared back. "You must hate people like me who profit from other's loss."

"You profited?"

"My company made me a wealthy man."

"Oh."

"But it will all be lost in the lawsuits, when they find the willful neglect of the higher ups in my company." His laugh was bitter. "My sons." He shook his head. "And I will not fight to keep it."

The story was beginning to come together. "What's your company's name?"

"Rose Prosthetics."

Cole tensed. He'd heard about the accident in the news. The victim was a decorated veteran and the head of a large family. His wife widowed, children orphaned, and all because this man's sons felt it more important to make a larger profit off the backs of the desperate. Bitterness swelled, peaked, then dissipated in one instant at the man's despondency.

Henry eyed Cole. "I can see you know the story."

"I do." Cole finished the coffee, his muscles dragging rather than holding him up. It'd been an exhausting evening, climbing those trails and rescuing Henry. Only now he wasn't so sure if he had been the rescuer? Yes, Cole had brought him to his home, but Henry had lent him his arm most of the trail leading there. He wasn't really sure who'd helped whom more.

Cole stood, leaning heavily on his crutch, wavering with the effects of the drink. "Mrs. Rivera will be down to show you to your room." He turned away.

"Why don't you use prosthetics, Cole?"

Cole stopped. The question stabbed him. The answer was none of this guy's business. Couldn't he see Cole's soul was too ugly to care about? The world should know this now more than ever.

"They could make your life much easier."

"Or kill me." Cole felt the man flinch without even seeing him. He regretted the words.

"Not all products are like what my sons built. We did a lot of good for a lot of people before they destroyed the company." He seemed to search for words. "My daughter is nothing like them. She's developed a new socket design that attaches closer to the bone from the outside. It could dramatically change the maneuverability for amputees who want to remain active. It's simple, but incredibly effective." He sucked in more air. "Only now, no one wants anything to do with the Rose family. She can't get any funding to develop the product. My lack of oversight of what my sons were doing has not only ruined her career, but also the future of a product that could help veterans like yourself."

"That's too bad." Cole couldn't control the self-pity that overtook him. "I'm sure she's as nice as a fairytale princess too." He thumped down the hall to his first-floor apartment and slammed the door.

~*~

Three months later ...

Carly Rose pulled up the long drive to the man's house. The forested lane opened, revealing—

Whoa! That was no house. It was more like a very expensive ski chalet. For hordes of guests. What did one man need with all that space? Carly's family had some money, but this guy must be loaded.

She scanned the circular drive. A young man in jeans and a t-shirt rubbed at the gleaming black limo inside an otherwise empty five-car garage. He leaned back and smiled at the shine he'd elicited.

Carly parked beside the front entrance and tried to blow the stray hair from her face. Soaked from the solid hour she'd just spent in the rain explaining to the roadside-assistance guy how to change her flat tire, the hair wouldn't budge.

Hoping Cole Harrison got the message she'd be late—very late—she glanced in the rearview to find a thick black smudge across her cheek. She rubbed. It held fast to her skin. Well, at least it matched the smears from the tire across her rain coat and blue jeans.

Thank goodness this was only an information session. Cole Harrison had finally agreed to try out her prototype prosthetics. It had taken her father much cajoling of the man over breakfast those many months ago, and repeated phone calls since. Why had Mr. Harrison resisted using prosthetics for so long? And why had he relented now? She shrugged. If he liked them, maybe he'd invest in a new company, giving at least part of the Rose family a chance at redemption.

"Am I okay here?" she called to the guy in the garage as she closed the door to her car.

His head bobbed, swinging his dark hair into his face. "Yup."

She poked the doorbell, straightened the still-damp shirt under her drenched raingear and waited. Her toe tapped with the nervous energy that buzzed through her. She fingered the gold cross at her neck.

A fiftyish woman opened the door. "Come in." She motioned for Carly to take off her coat. The woman called to the young man with a Hispanic lilt to her voice, "Beautiful, Manny. Mr. Cole will be very pleased."

Funny. When talking to her father, Carly got the idea that Cole Harrison was not one to be easily pleased. She'd asked her dad why he thought Mr. Harrison would invest in her designs and he'd answered with a far-away look and said, "I don't know, Carly. What other choices do we have?"

Choices. Was the only choice to start a new company? Did Carly want to run a business? That would mean more time with sales figures and less with clients. She didn't want to end up like her brothers, not caring for the people she served.

"Mr. Harrison will be right with you." The woman never asked Carly's name. He must not get many visitors out here.

Carly's gaze rolled over the expanse of the foyer, down several long halls decorated with gold-framed portraits and ornately carved tables, and into a living room housing couches littered with embroidered throw pillows.

The woman pointed. "Have a seat. Can I get you something to drink?"

Carly might have been soaked on the outside from standing in the rain, but the exertion of changing tires left her parched. "Water."

The woman nodded and hustled away.

Carly took a turn about the living room, running her finger along the mantel above the fireplace, noting the crystal set atop it. Pricey. Her eyes drew up to catch her reflection in the mirror above. Wet, straggly blond hair, wrinkled top, black smudges hither and yon—she looked like a mongrel dog. Or maybe the forest animal the mongrel caught up in his teeth. She chuckled. A step up from the ordinary that usually identified her.

Rhythmic thumping and clanging sounded from behind. It stopped. "You're quite the Beauty."

Carly pivoted to see the source of the sarcasm-laden tone, catching sight of the man missing alternate limbs, leaning on a metal crutch. Dark circles ringed his eyes and a scar split the left side of his closely-shaved head.

His gaze scanned her attire with a smirk. "Your father never mentioned you were so ... lovely. A fashion plate."

She stifled a comeback about his own appearance, but chose the higher road. "My father never mentioned you were such a wit."

His eyes widened and his lips almost twisted into something one might call a smile.

"Did you get my message?"

He hobbled closer. "Yes. Something about waiting on roadside assistance to change your tire." His gaze rolled over her. "It appears you didn't wait."

She pulled a packet of papers from her case and sat in an armchair. "How about we get started?"

"Certainly." He dropped into the overstuffed sofa.

"I have a number of questions I need you to answer, forms for you to fill out and I'll need to tour the manor's exercise facilities."

"Of course."

"Once you're fitted with the prosthetics, we'll begin rehab." She organized papers on the coffee table.

"Who'll be doing the fitting?"

"I will."

He stared. Was he looking at her or the wall behind her? His arrogance dripped from him like an oozing sore.

"I assure you, I am skilled both as a prosthetist and a physical therapist. I wanted to know all aspects of my field in order to get my designs right."

"Would you like to see your room?"

Was he even listening to her?

"Yes. As I mentioned, I'd like to tour the manor's exercise rooms. I assume that's where most of the rehab will take place."

"Not for rehab. Your apartment." His eyes were a steely blue, softened only by his thick lashes. It seems those and his eyebrows were the only hair he allowed on his entire head.

"My apartment?" Her heart beat against her chest. What had her father signed her up for? How desperate was he to land this investor?

"Yes, upstairs, where you'll be living for the next several months."

Carly placed the pen atop some papers and fingered her cross necklace.

"Didn't your father mention my expectation that rehab be daily? He said you live two hours away."

Carly thought of the lonely drive up the forested mountain road. She suspected there were few, beyond the wildlife, who actually lived within two hours of this place.

"I won't have you working with me exhausted after a long drive," Cole's eyelids hung as though he were bored, "possibly losing tires along the way."

She took in several cycles of breaths, gauging his expression. Could she trust this man—to live with him—in such a remote location? He was a complete stranger to her. An obviously bitter one. She thought about her father's excitement at the prospect of an interested investor. She knew her father's car hadn't met the tree only because of a storm. He'd gone out looking for death. And this hairless man offered him a chance at life.

Why?

"You'll have several rooms to yourself—a bathroom, kitchenette, patio and office. But I will expect you to eat dinner with me every evening."

Her eyebrows shot up of their own volition. "With my imprisonment here, this is beginning to sound like a dark retelling of a Disney flick."

His blink was heavy. "You mean Beauty and the Beast?"

She shrugged.

His lips curled higher. "I guess that makes me the Beauty."

Insolent man.

His tone grew serious. "I suggested you live here for a number of reasons. First," he ticked off a finger from his intact hand, "you live too far away. Second," he ticked off another finger, "we will need lots of time for rehab sessions. Third," his ring finger joined the others, "I'll want to process how things are going with the product at dinnertime. After all, I may be sinking a load of dough into it eventually."

Carly looked around, wondering how much of that "dough" he'd actually miss.

"And lastly," he placed his hand on the stump of his left leg, "given your family's recent dealings," he hesitated, likely for effect, "you will need to earn my trust."

Her fingers balled. "Earn your trust?" The words came out in force. She almost growled, holding in the names she wanted to heap at him. Maybe she was the beast. But he was right. He had no reason to trust her family and more reason not to. Both as a client and an investor.

She wished she could wash away the stain of what her brothers had done to her father's business. It didn't matter he'd had an impeccable reputation for years. All people would remember is how it ended. She had to change that with something new. Cole Harrison was the means with which to do that.

But would she be safe living under the same roof as him?

He must have read the question on her face. "You may call a locksmith to come and change the locks to all your rooms—my expense."

She speared him with her eyes. Carly never liked people answering the thoughts she hadn't voiced.

"And Mrs. Rivera will be here with you, not to mention the rest of the manor staff."

"Yes, I will." Did Mrs. Rivera appear at his word? She placed a tray with plates of cookies, a soda and a glass of water on the table between them.

She looked harmless enough.

Carly would do anything for her father. Especially after her brothers had destroyed his dream. She needed to rebuild it, even if it meant taking some risks. Someone needed to look out for him. "When do I move in?"

"As soon as you wish."

~*~

Cole liked this woman. She'd taken every inch of him in when she first turned his way, and never flinched. Must be a hazard of the trade—seeing limbless, disfigured wretches on a regular basis.

Not a trace of pity in her eyes. Good. He deserved none. He wasn't the hero.

Carly also had a spark of something else. A hint of spice. Cole liked spice. Too bad spice didn't like him back. Nothing could.

Should he have Jurvis look into her? His man-of-business, who sensed the housing bust months before it happened, had a financial sense none could match. Jurvis could smell a parasite a mile away.

Not necessary. Cole could figure this one out. Either her products worked or they didn't. He'd give her the opportunity to prove herself. Nothing more. Nothing less.

Besides, Carly intrigued him. The only time she'd flinched during their meeting was at the moment he'd mentioned her looks. What had she been thinking? Did it bother her that she was plain? Had her vanity been pierced? He regretted his sarcastic jabs once the totality of them tumbled from his lips. It's what made the men of his Marine unit hate him.

All, but one.

He'd vowed to become more likeable after the IED, but it was too late. His looks had been the only thing that attracted people to him before, especially women. Now his appearance matched what had always been inside—useless flesh.

Chapter Two

The ornately carved mahogany door opened in front of Carly.

"Hola, Ms. Rose." Mrs. Rivera's eyes twinkled as she gestured for Carly to enter. "Are you moving in today?"

"No, but I've brought a few things with me. They're in my car. I've also come to get a casting of Mr. Harrison's residual limbs. It's how I make the socket fit him properly for the new prosthetics."

"Ah. Our Beauty is here." The sardonic tone echoed through the long hall.

Carly rolled her eyes and turned to him. So she'd never have the model looks of her brothers' wives, but did this man need to continually mock her?

Cole Harrison hobbled closer. "You're looking tidier today. No tires to change?"

Her faux-smile muscles ached from overuse. "Mr. Harrison, I—"

"Please, call me Cole. Think of yourself as a guest here."

Funny. That was not at all how she'd characterize their relationship. "Cole," she said with special emphasis, "I believe I mentioned you'd need to wear shorts for the visit when I called earlier."

His brows drew together. He looked down to the slacks that, no doubt, Mrs. Rivera had ironed that morning. "Of course." Did he just stammer? His turn was too wobbly, like he'd done it more quickly than he ought. He righted his balance and limped away.

"Let me show you to your room." Mrs. Rivera hurried up a long, curving staircase. "I'll have Manny, the chauffer, bring your things from the car."

Carly shook her head. "No need to trouble him. I can handle it."

The housekeeper chuckled. "Trust me, it's no trouble. El chico es probably looking for an excuse to pull his head out of a college text. It's a wonder how much he's paid. Mr. Cole rarely leaves the estate."

"Then why does he keep a chauffeur?"

Mrs. Rivera continued down a long hall of the upper floor. "Mr. Cole hasn't driven since he lost his limbs. Although, I suspect, it gives him cause to provide the homeless college boy a place to live until he earns his online degree."

Homeless boy? Could the ogre have an actual, beating heart?

They traveled on. The lush carpet stretched before them. How long was this hall?

Mrs. Rivera seemed to read Carly's mind. "This mansion was built by Cole's *abuelo*—I'm sorry, *grandfather*—with the express intention of entertaining a large number of guests over a period of days. Your suite was for the most honored—movie stars, political people and the like." Nearing the end of the hall she pointed to a door. "This used to be the master suite. Only Mr. Cole doesn't use it. He doesn't like the stairs, so he's refurbished his father's old study past the kitchen on the first floor for his bedroom."

She turned. "And if you hear the scr—I mean, him calling out in the middle of the night, just ignore it, por favor. He's just having one of his nightmares."

Nightmares? Carly's mind conjured dark forests, full moons and shrieking goblins. She shivered the images away.

Mrs. Rivera pushed open a door across from the master suite. "The locksmith will be here shortly to install the locks, bolts, chains—anything you desire—and give you a key."

Carly scanned the expansive suite. "That isn't necessary. I could have—"

"Oh, no. He inseested."

Carly liked the way Mrs. Rivera's accent intensified when she became adamant.

"Mr. Harrison thinks people fear him because of his looks. He wants—no, needs—to put your mind at ease."

Carly marveled at the state-of-the art refrigerator and stove on one side of the apartment. Was this what he called a kitchenette? "Has anyone ever mentioned to him it's his winning personality that sets our hearts a-flutter?"

Mrs. Rivera's lips twitched. "Jes, jes, my dear. He is well aware he turns people away. But now he sees his looks and demeanor as one and the same."

Now?

She patted Carly's arm. "Somehow I think you will be very good for him." Was she talking about the prosthetics?

Mrs. Rivera hustled out into the hall. "Now let me show you how to get to the exercise facility from here."

Carly ran to keep up as the woman traveled the vast floor space. Until she learned the way, she'd need a tour guide. She didn't want to open the wrong door somewhere and find a chamber of secret horrors. She giggled at her over-active imagination until she remembered Mrs. Rivera's words. Unease slithered up her spine. What kind of nightmares did the likes of Cole Harrison experience?

~*~

Cole took a swig from his thermos. His Coke had just the right zing from the Vodka he'd been spiking it with. He could feel the constant tease of gunfire and explosives fade as the liquid fire descended his esophagus. Sweet relief.

The Rose woman entered carrying a tray topped with gauze rolls, a tape measure, a pen and a sweating can of soda. Mrs. Rivera hustled in close behind.

The housekeeper patted the cushion of the therapy table that woman insisted he purchase. "Have a seat, Mr. Cole."

A crazy metal contraption sat beside it, looking like a torture device used to rip out body parts.

Mrs. Rivera opened an overhead cabinet and pulled out some towels. She stood waiting patiently as the Rose woman knelt on the floor and arranged her utensils by his one, intact foot.

What was her first name again? Some days his hippocampus just didn't want to work at all. He absently touched the scar near his left temple. He'd already forgotten about the need to wear shorts and now even her first name was beyond reach. All he could pull up was an image of the Disney princess in the yellow ball gown.

"Beauty."

She jerked her attention to him, her eyes burning.

"Now, Carly, don't you mind him." Mrs. Rivera to the rescue—always knowing when he needed help with a name.

"That's okay, Mrs. Rivera. It's only that I'm a little confused. Last week, it seemed, Cole had our roles reversed."

"Ah, yes, but I think I've changed my mind. Beauty didn't really suit me. I think I'll let you keep it."

Carly sat back on her heels and took a sip of her soda. "After I take some measurements, we'll fit you into the imager over there to get a sense of the general shape of your leg." She gestured to the torture device. "Then, I'll apply the plaster and put you in it again allowing time for it to harden into a cast."

"Yes, Beauty." He liked to watch the fire ignite in her when he used the moniker. It distracted his mind from his more life-threatening imaginings.

She held fast to the soda can with her left hand as she picked up the tape measure in her right. What was that look on her face? He didn't trust it. She placed the soda on the floor and palmed his thigh.

"Argh!" Cole thrust her backwards. "Your hands are like ice."

Carly only smiled as she blew into her fists. Mrs. Rivera placed the towels beside the ice queen and chuckled. "I'll leave you now. It appears you can handle Mr. Cole on your own." Her mocking laughter trailed her down the hall.

Cole's nostrils flared as he struggled to recover his breath. "You did that on purpose."

His forehead tensed. "Please do not handle that soda can until you are done here."

Carly's fingers, only slightly warmer now, probed the bony structure of his thigh and stretched the tape measure around it. She didn't make eye contact. "Well, at least we know the nerves in your limb are working." Her lips tugged up. "Quite well in fact."

Cole was not appeased. He pulled at the nozzle on his thermos and sucked down a few gulps of his brew. Why did he agree to try these fake limbs again? He'd hated the ones he'd had before. The image of Henry's eyes as he pleaded with Cole to give them a chance softened his ire. It was more than a business proposition. To one of them, he sensed, it meant life.

"Why do you get to drink and I don't?" Her eyebrows held a challenge.

Cole's limbs, residual and otherwise, began to feel heavier. "Because you will use your icy fingers as a weapon, whereas I," he wiggled his right-arm stump, "cannot."

Carly pulled him to stand and led him to the imager device. She mumbled something about the IED missing his tongue, but he couldn't hear the particulars.

"Stand up straight and tall." She fitted the residual of his left thigh into the machine and closed the metal bars at every angle around it until they pressed tightly into his femur. The rods against his skeleton gave him an immediate sense of security and stability. Good thing, because the drink had been making him less so.

She smiled, eying his expression. "How does it feel?"

"Good."

"You need to give me more than that. Does it pinch too hard?"

He shook his head. "Not at all. Each rod seems to push the fatty tissue and flesh away so as not to pinch."

Her expression told Cole she was pleased with herself. "That's exactly what we're looking for." She tapped at a rod. "Does it feel connected?"

He drew his brows together and considered the sensations of his skin, the firmness of the attachment and even a new relationship to gravity. "Yes. Very connected. Almost like to the bone itself."

Her self-satisfied grin grew. "Good. We want it to feel like a part of you rather than something moving around the outside of your flesh."

Cole nodded, but didn't say anything. Something ran through him like the faint flicker of hope, but he pushed it away. He knew what hope had always wrought. He wasn't going there ever again. He drew from his drink, his muscles weakening as he did.

She loosened him from the device, allowing him to remove his leg. "Now I'll need to plaster the limb, then put you back in while it hardens into a mold."

"Plasther?" His tongue was getting heavy now.

Carly's face tensed. "Yes. To make the socket." Her gaze traveled to the left side of his skull. "What other injuries did you suffer from the IED?"

"The oneths you see—only." He struggled to work his tongue more precisely over the words.

"You need to tell me everything. It may be important to your rehab."

"There's nothing else."

She pointed to his scar. "How about your head? Her eyes moved as if she were going over events in her mind. "Have you suffered any memory loss? Short-term? Name retrieval?"

Didn't she have enough? Did she need to demean him further? "No." He drew from the thermos longer this time. His eyelids fell as he swallowed.

He opened them to find Carly's focus zeroed in on his face, but her gaze traveled with the thermos, as he placed it on the therapy table.

"What's in that drink?"

"Soda."

"What else?" She became more annoying with each tick of the wall clock.

"Nothing." He looked past her. "Mrs. Rivera!" he called over her shoulder.

Carly's jaw almost crackled with tension.

"Mrs. Rivera!"

The housekeeper hustled into the room. "Jes, Mr. Cole."

He held out the thermos. "Please take this to the kitchen. It's apparently distracting our Beauty here. She's jealous because I won't let her drink her own."

Mrs. Rivera turned to Carly then back to Cole, seeming to find answers to the question in her eyes. The housekeeper knew what was in that bottle having been there when he'd mixed it. She grasped the canister and scurried out.

Why did it feel as though his body-armor had been ripped from him in the middle of a fire-fight?

Carly slapped his residual leg. "Stand up straight, Marine. No slacking." She dipped the wrap in some water, then unwound it around his limb. Her fingers worked the plaster into the landscape of his tissues. She focused all attention on her work—smoothing, pushing, deepening. Her fingers were strong. She left no detail unattended.

"So what types of activities would you most like to regain with your new prosthetics." She seemed to speak only to his leg now.

"Who says I want to regain any of my old life." He felt like sludge. It became harder and harder to stay focused.

"Did you hike, ski, um…" Carly swallowed, "…horseback ride?" She must have talked to Mrs. Rivera.

"Yes."

"Which one?"

"All of them." Did she need to tax his mind as well as his limbs?

"Since I'll be working as your physical therapist it's helpful to know what activities you enjoyed. It gives us goals to work toward—things that might encourage you to try harder."

Cole wasn't sure if it was the alcohol or not, but he drew a blank when it came to enjoyment—real enjoyment. Yes, things had made him happy in the past, but they always seemed fleeting. He'd often been looking for that next great thing that would make his life worthwhile.

His mind traveled unbidden to visions of Beckett, but these were not of bloodshed and body parts, as most often saturated his dreams. The pimply-faced Marine rarely wore anything but a smile on his lips. Cole had often wondered at his mental capacity. No sane person could be that happy. Cole had almost envied him the inanity. But Beckett was far from simple. In fact, he sometimes seemed to … know things. Things about Cole he'd never shared with anyone—his emptiness, his longing for more.

"I believe Mrs. Rivera told me you still hike." Carly's words dragged him from the quicksand of his mind.

He nodded.

"That's how you found my father." The pressure of her fingers into the muscles of his leg almost soothed him. She unwound another layer of the plaster-coated bandage around the limb. "What were you doing out in the middle of a blizzard?"

He tensed.

Her eyes seem to probe into his thoughts. What was she looking for? Her expression softened. What had she found?

No, no, no. Not the pity. "I was looking for idiots who chose to drive recklessly during a snowstorm."

She straightened.

"One is bound to find one on a night like that."

She rolled another layer and worked it deeper into his soft tissue—a little too deep this time. He stifled the wince.

Had he gone too far? A woman can be very protective of her father. He sucked in a breath and whispered, "Horseback riding."

She stopped her work, but did not meet his gaze. Her hand went to the gold necklace dangling from her throat—a cross. Was she holding her breath?

He was, because in that moment, it became clear. He knew what he most wanted to regain. "I'd like to ride a horse again."

Chapter Three

Carly palmed the keys the locksmith had given her for her suite … or apartment … or however one would describe her living arrangement inside this mansion.

The works. That's what she'd call the myriad of locks he'd installed. Doorknob, deadbolt, and one of those bar thingies she'd only seen in hotel rooms. Tom Cruise, hanging by a wire in form-fitting ebony, couldn't gain entry.

She turned to leave and almost ran into a walking shelf unit.

"Sorry, Carly." Manny spoke through the slats of the small piece of furniture he carried. "Mr. Cole wanted you to have this for your room." He smirked. "I told him about the boxes of books I brought in this morning."

Carly could never part with her books. She'd moved out of the apartment she'd lived in, but couldn't bear to put her favorites in storage. She never knew which "old friend" would come in handy to take her mind off her troubles. "Sorry, Manny, I didn't mean for you to carry all those."

"Oh, no trouble."

She eyed him with a crooked smile. "Only enough to mention it to your boss."

Manny placed the furniture on the floor with a grunt. "That's only 'cause he asked what you might need."

Carly looked around the room at the various appliances, wide-screen T.V., DVD-player, and comfy living-room furniture. "Well, it looks like I have everything now."

"Great." He waved. "See ya later. Gotta make a run for Mr. Cole."

"A run?"

"Oh, uh, the store."

Hmmm. Manny didn't seem the grocery-shopping type.

After locking her suite, she trudged the long hall, descended the curving staircase and continued toward the lower patio door behind the breakfast room. What a trek. She stepped out and followed the worn path she knew, by the view from her apartment, would take her to the stable. Now, she needed to muster a little courage to enter.

As Carly opened the doorway to the wooden structure, the smells of hay, manure and leather enveloped her. The grit kicked up from the dirt floor already began to coat her skin and fill her lungs. A diminutive man with graying hair and crinkles around his Asian features turned from brushing a shiny black horse. Carly halted.

That was one large animal at his side. She'd forgotten how big those beasts could be.

"May I help you?" His voice didn't hold any of the Asian accent she'd expected. He stepped toward her, and the animal moved with him.

Carly fingered the gold cross at her neck. "Um ..." She backed up, then watched the beast to make sure he stayed put. "My name is Carly Rose."

The man's smile held humor. "Oh yes, you've come to help Mr. Cole with the new prosthetics." He thumped the side of the horse. "You hear that, Lightning?"

The horse whinnied.

Carly kept the animal in her sights. Lightning. Of course it had a deadly name.

The man looked between Carly and Lightning as though she and the horse had a history—and he needed to learn it. His brows scrunched. "I'm Joe Sakamoto." He reached out a hand. The horse shook his head and Carly jumped.

Joe chuckled. "She won't bite."

She?

Carly wasn't taking chances. She watched Lightning closely while shaking the man's hand. "While prepping for rehab, we like to have goals our clients can work toward—something meaningful that will encourage them to work through the rough spots." She glanced at the animal. Its muscles bulged. Hers tensed.

Joe grimaced.

"Cole said he'd like to ride a horse again."

Shock. Joe could have caught flies, his mouth dangled open so long. "He did?"

"Yes."

"He can do that now. He doesn't need prosthetics. I've told him that before."

Carly almost forgot the horse. Almost. "Then why doesn't he ride?"

Joe threw the brush into a bin. "Have you seen the scar on his face and head?" His chuckle was sullen. "Of course you have. He displays it like a gothic movie billboard." Joe glanced to her as he took the reins of the horse and led her into a stall. "That wasn't from the IED that took his limbs."

Did she hear him right?

Joe stepped from the stall and closed the door. "That was from his attempt to ride the first week he'd gotten home."

"What?" She was hating this horse idea more and more. "But you said he could ride now."

"Sure, but he needs to relearn how to ride with his new body. The balance and control will be entirely different. He'll need to start slow and have an equine occupational therapist work with him and train the horse." He clapped the dust from his hands. "We'll also have to build him a platform so he can mount the horse properly—not finagle his way on by way of a rickety fence, then gallop off at top speed."

Carly gasped. "He didn't."

Joe nodded. "Drinking a pint of whiskey beforehand didn't help."

Her heart pounded as though she'd been racing with him. Her mind drew up the silver thermos Cole had in the manor gym. She'd wondered what was in it. Now she had more evidence her suspicions were correct.

"He fell on a large rock and damaged his skull."

She pivoted. "No. This is not a good idea."

"Actually, it's the best idea."

Carly turned back.

"Mr. Cole loved to ride more than anything since he was a little boy. It was the only thing that brought him joy." The man's features softened. "He spent much of his day here with me when his parents went out of town." He leaned against the wood-plank wall. "Mr. Cole should ride again. You'll be doing a good thing. He just needs to be re-taught how."

"Why didn't he ask someone to help him?"

Joe almost doubled over with laughter. "You've met the man, haven't you?"

Of course she had. Carly shifted her stance, her tennis shoes kicking up sand.

Mirthful pity etched the wrinkles around Joe's eyes. "He's not one for slow. And even worse, he doesn't like to have others in control. That's why he made sure to graduate college before joining the Marines. He needed to become an officer and did whatever he could to gain a position of authority."

"He was an expert rider as a young man." Joe gestured toward a shelf with his chin. "Won all those trophies over there." He mumbled, "Though his parents never took notice." His voice rose again. "For him, humbling himself in order to relearn something he'd already known so well will take everything he has. You'll have your work cut out for you."

"Me?" Her heart whammed against her sternum. "I thought you'd help with the riding."

"Oh, no."

Oh, no was right!

"I was talking about getting him up here to start again. He hasn't even come to see Lightning since he fell. My son can help with the riding. He's an occupational therapist and works using horses. I think he calls it hippotherapy."

"Cole says he wants to ride again."

Joe shook his head. "I don't know how you got him to want anything. I've tried for years. But I suspect saying it and allowing himself the joy of it will be two totally different things."

Allowing joy? What kind of sadist was she moving in with? What had her father gotten her into? The challenges of this job seemed to grow and entangle like a virulent weed.

The whinnies of two other horses caught Carly's attention. "Why does he keep the horses if he doesn't ride?"

Joe thrust a thumb toward the animals. "Those two were his parents' horses. His fondest memories of them—if one could call them fond—were when they'd agreed to ride with him. When they died he couldn't lose the only connection to them he'd ever known."

Carly couldn't imagine. She'd relished the memories she had with her own parents. Had Cole Harrison had any of that? Carly's hand reached again for the cross necklace her mother had given her on her fourteenth birthday.

She wanted to know more. "How'd they die?"

"Nine-eleven. They were in the first plane to hit the towers." He paused. "Cole hadn't even known they'd been in the country when Jurvis, the family's lawyer, showed up at his dorm-room door to inform him they were dead and he'd inherited the estate."

The dirt in the air seemed to grow heavy inside her lungs.

"He labored through his last semester of school and joined the Marines immediately after." Joe pushed his hands in his worn jeans pockets. "I think he felt the only way to fill the gaping hole inside him was to even the score."

"The score?"

"Between him and the terrorists." He gestured to the necklace in Carly's fingers. "Of course we both know there's only one way to fill that kind of hole."

Chapter Four

Did Cole have a beating heart behind each eyeball? Or a ticking time bomb?

He rubbed at his forehead, his temples, then palmed his eyes, but nothing lessened the throb.

He scanned the empty patio, pulled in a lungful of fresh mountain air, then extricated the flask from his back jeans pocket and emptied it into his orange juice.

"Morning sustenance, Mr. Cole?"

Cole hated the way Joe Sakamoto used the title *Mr.* ever since Cole inherited the estate. Their relationship had once been that of mentor and protégé—almost father and son. Mr. Sakamoto had not only taught Cole expert horsemanship, he'd counseled him on the things a man needs to know as he matures. Even taught him how to shave. Then Joe had become distant when Cole hit his late teens, not at the stables as much. Feeling rejected, Cole had abandoned the things Joe taught him for the partying life and hobnobbing with the rich and famous he thought his parents would admire.

Now Joe deferred to him as Mr. Cole. He'd relish the authority over anyone else, but with Joe it was like he'd built a wall in their relationship that never could be breached.

Cole shoved the flask into his back jeans pocket. "If you had to deal with that Rose woman, you'd want something to melt the edge too."

Joe's eyebrows lifted. "You mean Carly?"

Carly. Why did her name keep slipping from him? The only names he could hold were the ones he'd attached to visual images. Her last name—Rose—and the yellow ball-gown-wearing Disney princess—Beauty. The neurologist had told him he'd need to use pictures to remember things. He wasn't kidding

"Yes." Cole closed his eyes against the pain. "Her."

Joe's scraping of the wrought-iron chair against the slate sent glass shards through Cole's brain.

He sat across from Cole, the ever-present lilt to his lips. "She seemed very pleasant to me."

"When did you meet her?" Why did Cole's pulse kick up at the thought of them talking? He took a long draw of the doctored juice.

Joe's eyes seemed to hold a question ... or was that a challenge? "Last time she was here she said you wanted to ride a horse again."

Did the woman have to take his whispered words so seriously? "I said that to shut her up." He twisted the OJ glass back and forth on the table. "She kept pestering me about goals." He shrugged. "Then I insulted her father—"

Joe's mock gasp made Cole flinch. "You?" His eyes held the humor Cole had remembered as a boy.

Cole slid him a snide smile. "Yes, me. So I told her about the riding."

"Do you?" The man stared. Joe's eyes always had a way of reaching into Cole's soul. One reason he'd avoided the stables for so long.

"Yes, yes." Cole hated to admit defeat. "I'd like to ride again."

Joe's chair scooched across the slate as he stood. "Great. I'll tell my son."

Cole sighed. "The occupational therapist?" The idea of relearning riding from some young punk weighed on him.

"Yes. And we'll get Carly to be a side-walker."

This was sounding slower and slower every minute. He just wanted to mount his steed and blow like the wind, climb old hills and jump wide hedges. The idea of a side walker made it sound more like a mosey and less like a ride. "I don't need a side walker."

"You need to start slow and have someone at each side until you regain a proper sense of balance."

Cole harrumphed.

"But if it makes you feel any better," the spark in Joe's eyes was devilish, "she's deathly afraid of horses." Joe turned and strode toward the stable with what appeared to be a new sense of purpose.

Carly? Afraid of horses?

Cole leaned back in the patio chair, a smile tugging at one side of his lips. He couldn't imagine her afraid of anything, but the thought of dangling her kryptonite in front of her made the idea of riding—even at an excruciatingly slow pace—all the more interesting. And Joe seemed to know that. Did Joe have lessons in mind for her as well? What was he up to? Cole almost wanted to find out.

The French doors opened behind him. Mrs. Rivera peaked through. "Carly is here, Mr. Cole. She is moving the last of her things in this morning and expects to have a fitting appointment with you in one hour." She waved a kitchen towel. "Something about a check socket."

Cole knew what that meant. He'd traveled this road at the VA. "Tell her I'll meet her in the gym."

Mrs. Rivera closed the door.

"And I'll wear my shorts," he called out, not really caring if anyone heard. He was just glad he'd remembered himself.

~*~

The gym teetered a little as Cole hobbled in. He held onto the new weight machine he'd ordered at Carly's suggestion. The place was beginning to look like a real rehab center, even if it did buck and sway in his inebriated state.

She had two chairs set up next to the parallel bars, a small fitting stand between them and a couple of clear plastic frames on the floor. Those must be the check sockets. Very different from the plastic buckets he'd remembered from his past prosthetics. This was the appointment where she'd stick those on his residual limbs, check the fit—he'd stand, sit, stand, sit, roll over, beg. He shook his head at the image.

Interminable and boring.

He hadn't brought his thermos, or his flask, to this appointment—he didn't want to raise the lady's ire—so he made sure to fill up on the drink before he got there.

His eyelids weighed heavy as though his lashes were made of lead.

Carly stood and turned. The movement in his field of vision made him dizzy. He wavered, the crutch not seeming to do its job keeping him up.

"You're drunk." Oh well, it seems her ire was there anyway.

He said nothing. Couldn't really think of what to say. He plopped into one of the chairs and stuck out the left residual stump. "Go ahead, put it on."

She just stared.

"The socket thing." Didn't she know what he meant?

Her nostrils flared. Cole imagined steam rising from them. He couldn't help but laugh at the idea she reminded him of a dragon.

Her eyebrows crunched. Uh-oh, he'd never seen that look before.

"I will not work with you while you're drinking." She stood.

He rose and reached after her. "Hey. Come on."

She yanked out of his grasp. He stumbled, but the metal crutch couldn't brace his fall. His face hit the padded floor.

Beauty turned back. "Sober up, Cole, or I walk."

He rolled over and rubbed the knot on his forehead. "Can you at least help me up, please?"

"No." She stared ice-daggers.

He released a deep sigh and lifted himself off the floor. "Fine." He plopped into the chair. "I'll be sober by this evening. We can do your little fitting then."

"No."

His gaze met her dark burning eyes.

"You will be sober for one full week before I work with you."

Cole's breathing labored. His heart thumped. Did that scare him? "Why a week?"

Her voice was strained but firm. "I need your full attention, and every nerve working in order to fit the sockets to your limbs correctly. You will need to be able to confirm to me every discomfort, pinch or slight gap. Otherwise the socket will rub and burn. You need to be able to feel it."

He shrugged. "But why a week?"

Her expression told Cole she knew more than she should. "Because I don't want to begin the work, and especially not the therapy, before the DTs have come and gone."

The DTs. Delerium Tremens. The words shook through his body as though he were experiencing them now. He closed his eyes trying to block the thought. It didn't work.

He couldn't go through that again. When Joe had challenged him years ago after he'd landed in the hospital from the effects of a virulent frat party he thought he'd die. The shaking, the vomiting, the feeling of bugs crawling all over his body, the crazy hallucinations. He'd stayed sober for two months before his parents were killed. They'd never even known he'd had a drinking problem.

He'd even remained sober through years of Marine officer training. But then he'd gone to war—war with guns, bombs and body counts. Drinking seemed his only cure.

Now this Rose woman wanted to take that away and subject him to that hell again.

He looked at her to find her eyes taking in every detail of his expression. Her gaze seemed to search deep into his mind, her features softening to ... what?

Pity. He didn't need her pity!

"Fine." He bit into the words. "I'll be sober for a week."

~*~

Carly tromped down the hall, passed the office, the library, the theatre room and all the rooms in between.

He'll be sober for a week. What did that mean? Did he think he could start drinking again at the clanging of the clock?

Carly entered the kitchen. "Mrs. Rivera?"

The woman pivoted, a plastic bag of bread in her hands, questions in her eyes.

"We need to rid this house of all the possible alcohol that your employer has, including anything he may have hidden."

Her mouth dropped open, the bag of bread now dangling.

"Cole has agreed to be sober."

Mrs. Rivera's eyes did not register anything resembling belief.

Carly opened cabinets above the counters, grabbed some Jim Beam, opened and dumped its contents into the sink. She searched the cabinets below. "We need to remove any temptation, otherwise—"

"Whoa! What are you doing?"

Mrs. Rivera gasped at her employer's voice.

Cole hobbled in. "This is my house and you do not order my staff to remove my possessions without my say."

Carly sucked in a deep breath. "You cannot resist alcohol if it's staring you in the face."

He glanced around, and shrugged. "I don't see its beady eyes anywhere."

She stepped within two feet of him and looked up into his face. She hadn't realized how tall he was until that moment. "But you know exactly where it is."

His jaw jerked.

"Where is it?"

He didn't budge.

She pivoted toward Mrs. Rivera, still by the counter as though she'd eyed Medusa. "Do you know?"

Mrs. Rivera turned toward Cole.

"Don't bring her into this." Cole's deep voice rained down on Carly.

She stifled a shudder, stepped back, and gestured around. "Every one of your staff is part of this if they know where you keep your bottles or can be convinced to buy you more."

Cole's brow bunched and his crutch hit the floor with force as he moved closer. "Have you forgotten your father's business needs me," he thumped his chest with his right-arm stump, "as an investor?"

Carly shifted her weight. She knew this fire could scorch if she didn't play carefully.

"I did not ask for this. I did not want this." The scar at his lip jumped with the force of his words.

"Then why did you agree to it?"

His lips pressed into a thin line.

Carly closed her eyes. None of this made sense. She'd felt from the beginning he didn't really want to try the prosthetics, yet here he was, virtually supporting her as he did.

Why?

It was for that reason her father owed Cole his life, but— "How can you endorse a product that does not work for you because you were too drunk to feel your limbs enough to get a proper fit?"

"I told you I'll be completely sober by this evening?"

"And what do you think would happen, Cole," his name came out through gritted teeth, "if the press got wind of a tragic accident involving my new prosthetics? One which could have been prevented if the recipient had been sober?"

Cole's gaze fell to his one shoe.

"No, Cole. I'd rather not have an investor who's more likely to sabotage the product."

Cole continued to view the floor for several heart beats. Carly could barely control the thrumming in her chest. Her eyes stung. She didn't know why this bothered her so much. Yes, she wanted to rebuild her father's dream, but something told her there was more.

She stared at the shell of a man who'd given limbs for her country and swallowed the lump in her throat.

His gaze rose to hers. "You're right." His voice was barely audible. "Mrs. Rivera, remove all the liquor from the cabinets."

The housekeeper put the bread on the counter and opened several cabinets filled with bottles.

"I'll get my personal stash." He pivoted toward the hall.

"Personal stash?"

"In my suite." He thumped a few more steps toward his bedroom. "See you at dinner."

Chapter Five

Carly flattened the last box used to move her stuff into her new apartment and blew the mousey blonde strays from her ponytail out of her face. She'd worked up a good sweat getting things in order before meeting Cole in the manor dining room.

Shocked he still expected her appearance at dinner after their clash this morning, her nerves buzzed through her like a chainsaw. She wondered why he expected it. Yes, she had agreed to talk with him each night about the product, but he hadn't used her prosthetics yet, so there was nothing to discuss. Would he quiz her on her business acumen to see if she could run a company? She hoped not. Her strength was in working with the amputees directly, and listening to their needs. The idea of taking her father's role only added to the weight she carried.

The glass-domed, gold clock on the mantle over the suite's fireplace chimed six times. Looks like she'd be late, given the ten minute walk from here to the other end of the manor. Carly checked her reflection, smoothed the stray hairs behind her ear, straightened her t-shirt over her "moving" jeans and headed down the hall.

She halted at the dining room. Not because of the extravagance of the crystal-dripping chandelier or the elegance of the linen-draped table surrounded by eight upholstered chairs.

What caught Carly's attention was the sight of Cole in a crisply ironed royal-blue dress shirt and tailored slacks pinned up on one knee. His attention rose from the book in front of him, long lashes lifting to reveal eyes that matched the color of his shirt. She could almost see the five o'clock shadow beginning to grow on his scalp. It gave a new shape to the solid lines of his face.

He scowled as she entered, bending the scar across his cheek, and deepening the dark circles under his eyes. "Your yellow ball gown at the cleaners?"

She rolled her eyes and flopped into the chair across from him. Was she supposed to feel self-conscious in her working clothes? Too bad. It wasn't her fault she hadn't gotten the dress-code memo.

Mrs. Rivera peeked in from the kitchen doorway. "You're here, Carly. I will serve you, ahora."

Cole thumped his book closed and pushed it aside. Mrs. Rivera entered bearing two plates. She placed one in front of each, between the ordered flatware and linen napkins. But there was no knife.

Steak. Already cut into little pieces. In fact, all the food had been cut as if she were a toddler needing her parent's permission to use a sharp object. She glanced at Cole, who heartily filled his mouth using his only hand. Mrs. Rivera must have cut Carly's so Cole wouldn't feel inferior.

Just as her eyes began to fill from the tenderness of Mrs. Rivera's care, Cole looked up at her. "Eat."

She picked up a fork and stacked a few green beans on the tines. "So what did you want to talk about?"

He shoveled food into his mouth. "Who says I wanted to talk."

"Isn't that why I'm to dine with you every night? To talk about the products?"

"I haven't tried them yet. What's there to say?"

"Then why … ?" She shook her head and took a bite of mashed potatoes.

The walls echoed the swooshing of the grandfather clock's pendulum and the dishes clanging in the kitchen next door. Carly shifted in her seat. Then shifted again. Why was she here?

"The house is clear," he said to his plate.

"Clear?"

"Of alcohol." His jaw grew ridged with the word.

"Good." Was that sweat on his brow? With the cranked up air conditioning she couldn't imagine how. He swiped his entire face with the linen napkin then scratched his residual arm like he couldn't make the itch go away.

The look of terror on his face this morning when she mentioned the DTs replayed in her mind. Carly thought she'd exaggerated the possibilities, not imagining he'd had enough of a drinking history to get them. But his expression told her he'd likely *been-there done-that*.

When she'd asked Joe about it, he'd turned white. "We'll need to be ready."

Carly asked what for, but he only replied, "Because he won't go into the hospital again unless he's unconscious and we take him."

The thought shook her. Was he really that stubborn? Or did he have a death wish?

What was she in for this week? She didn't want to know, but was certain she needed to see it through. She fingered the cross at her neck. Carly didn't just want her prosthetics to succeed. She was beginning to believe she also wanted this man to succeed.

The scratching stopped. Cole's gaze met hers. "What are you staring at?"

She dropped her attention to her plate. "Nothing."

"Then stop doing it." He glared at his milk as though willing it to be rum. "Eat your dinner. Mrs. Rivera has cake for dessert."

The woman appeared through the swinging doors. "Here we are."

Uncanny. Either his voice always conjured her or she listened at the doorway. Carly guessed the latter.

Mrs. Rivera set the plates loaded with chocolate cake and raspberry sauce in front of each. Cole's lips stretched into a boyish grin. It was almost ... sweet. "Thanks, Mrs. Rivera."

The lady nodded, a deep warmth in her large brown eyes. "De nada, Mr. Cole." She straightened. "Oh, did Manny thank you for helping him with his statistics homework? He got an A." She shook her head. "My nephew sometimes forgets his manners."

Cole's smile slid up on one side. "Yes he did, Auntie Rivera."

She headed toward the kitchen, then pivoted. "And thank you for taking care of—"

Cole waved her away. "You already thanked me for that, too." Cole's gaze traveled from the retreating housekeeper to Carly. "What?"

Who was this man? "What-what?"

His eyebrow lurched. "You're smirking."

"No, I'm not." She dug into the cake.

"Then what was that funny smile about?"

Had she been smiling? "I can't smile when someone brings me cake?"

"You weren't just smiling," Was he angry or amused? "You were smiling at me."

"That was your imagination."

The spark fled his eyes suddenly, and he scratched at his chest through his shirt.

Was the itch the beginning of the DTs—already? Her heart plunged at the reminder of the coming storm.

~*~

The manor had become unbearable for Carly. Cole's mood grew darker with each passing hour, and it seemed to permeate every nook and cranny—certainly all the staff. Joe's admonition to be ready echoed in her mind. Carly had eaten dinner the second evening only to meet with growls and unadulterated insults as he tore at his skin with his fingernails. On occasion, he seemed to reach for the arm that wasn't there. A phantom itch?

At least he had the sense not to expect her the third night. He'd eaten in his suite.

After he'd made even Mrs. Rivera cry with his harsh treatment, Carly retreated out of doors. She walked the property. The long tree-lined drive, the extensive, meandering gardens, the trails through the woods. She took a book and found places to read for long stretches of time.

She'd spent hours avoiding the house, but finally headed back, passing the stables—the harbinger of her future doom. That is, if she survived the current one.

She followed the worn path from the stable.

"Carly. Quick." Joe ran past her and continued as he called over his shoulder, "Mrs. Rivera just called me. Cole's having seizures."

Carly ran behind him, following to the house. Mrs. Rivera knelt in the living room by Cole's jerking and arching form, trying to control his flailing limbs.

A guilty weight fell over Carly. This was her doing. She'd challenged him as though it were the simplest thing in the world, not realizing the havoc she would cause all involved.

Cole growled foul verbiage as though possessed by demons. Mrs. Rivera prayed in shrieks of hysterics calling on saints Carly didn't know existed. Joe fell to his knees and held Cole's body to keep it from banging furniture, or inadvertently swatting poor Mrs. Rivera.

"Call 911." Joe struggled to speak.

Carly pulled out her cell, punched in the numbers and described the scene.

Cole's growls seemed to rumble from the bowels of Hades, laced with fire, singeing all they touched.

She ran to the foyer, opened the door, and waited for the rescue team. The sirens finally grew in volume, preceding the flashing lights and emergency medical team. Carly didn't know if it had taken five minutes or forty-five, but they were late as far as she was concerned.

The gurney appeared from the living room an unconscious, though still seizing, Cole lay atop it. Joe followed.

"I want to go with you." Carly couldn't just wait for word.

Joe hesitated.

"I want to be there. Make sure he's all right."

He nodded. "Come. I'll drive us."

They'd waited outside the emergency room until a woman in scrubs approached them. "He's stable and sedated for now. We'll need to admit him for several days to make sure he's safe."

Joe nodded. Carly fell into a waiting room chair.

"Carly, go back to the house and get some sleep. I'll call Manny."

"I want to be here when he wakes."

"That might not be for days, but someone should be here for him. I'll take tonight." He rested a hand on her shoulder. "You get some rest and come back in the morning."

"It's my fault," she said over a sob.

"You did the right thing challenging him, Carly. It's been a long-time coming. If he didn't stop soon, the end result would have been death. Unfortunately, the longer he took to climb this particular precipice the deeper the drop."

Chapter Six

Cole awoke to find himself in a hospital room. Through bleary eyes he scanned the space—light blue curtains, windows, sterile walls, beeping machines.

But no people. The room's emptiness echoed the sound of his heart monitor.

Why would anyone be here? He had no one who really cared.

The sun poured through the window, showering the space with a milky haze. The blood pressure cuff hummed and filled with air, strangling his left arm, then released. Cole watched the LED display numbers he couldn't read.

Someone cleared his throat. Cole's attention swung to the chair in front of his bed and the Marine who sat in full gear.

Beckett.

The heart monitor beeped a higher pace.

Beckett held his helmet in his lap. "How are you, sir?"

Cole scrubbed his face with his hand. "Fine." What else could he say?

Beckett stood and walked over to the bed. "I hear it's been rough since you got home." His face had a fierce sunburn that seemed too recent for the climate.

"Yeah."

"You always told us we could do anything if we put our minds to it." Was that a blister on his forehead?

Cole grunted. "After I called you a sack of sorry slugs." Most of his squad didn't like Cole's demeaning rages, but no matter what Cole did or said, Beckett strove to be better."

Beckett laughed. A scab on his lip cracked and bled.

Cole joined the laugh, but stopped. He needed to tell Beckett. "I owe you my life."

Was the blister on his head bubbling?

Beckett ran his palm across his cheek. A blood-red smear trailed its wake. His eyes intense. "I never wanted your life, sir."

Did his skin begin to sizzle? And the smell. Not that smell. Cole could not bear the smell of burning flesh.

Beckett leaned in close, his breath hot on Cole's face. " … I wanted your soul."

Beckett's form burst into flames that extinguished into black smoke. As the smoke cleared, blue ash rained over Cole's hospital blanket. Cole struggled to push the covers off, but he was tangled in them—one arm a useless stump, the other hung by a blood-pressure cuff.

Why couldn't he scream?

~*~

"Beckett, No!"

Carly startled awake in the chair she'd spent much of the past few days in. "Cole." She ran to the thrashing form and pushed the nurse's button. She held him down so he wouldn't hurt himself.

A nurse entered, taking his left side.

"He must be having a nightmare."

The nursed nodded. "Or hallucinations." She flexed to control him better.

Carly held Cole's right residual arm in both hands. She rubbed the limb, massaging it, hoping to calm him. She took in the landscape she'd come to know while making a plaster impression of it for the socket—where the muscle began and where it tapered off, the length of the bony structure below the elbow and the scar tissue at the end. She moved her fingers gently along the skin and into his soft tissue, then moved over his shoulder and messaged near his neck. His breathing relaxed and his heart monitor slowed.

Manny appeared in the doorway, eyes widening in horror as he took in the scene. An orderly ushered him from the entry. Carly's mind traveled to the conversations she'd had with Cole's unlikely chauffeur. Not quite the type one saw on TV, donned in a black uniform. Manny wore a t-shirt and holey jeans that contrasted the gleaming ebony vehicle he polished on a regular basis.

On the drives to and from the hospital each day, Manny had shared how Cole had taken him in after Manny's father had died of cirrhosis. Manny's gaze, in the rearview mirror of the limo, held a warmth, but humor, as he spoke of the curmudgeon who seemed to hide his acts of kindness as though they made him vulnerable. Carly's heart ached for the orphaned young man who'd lost his mother at six.

But what of the grouch who'd taken him in?

Carly turned to the man on the bed and brushed at the new growth of hair on his scalp. Cole's chest rose and fell, sucking in a large gulp of air through his nose. His eyes opened hard. He looked first to the nurse, then to Carly.

His features softened. "Beauty." The whispered words held none of the sarcasm she'd come to expect. She almost believed he meant it.

"I think he's stable now." The nurse patted his shoulder and turned. "Let me know if you need me again."

Cole's gaze fell to Carly's hands still running along his residual limb.

Feeling self-conscious, she removed them and stepped back.

"You smell like coconut."

He'd noticed her lotion?

"A welcome change."

Change from what?

His features pinched as if to stave off a horrific nightmare. He closed his eyes and drew in another breath. "Yes, coconut."

She didn't want to leave him there, but thought of the two men who'd been sitting in the waiting room each day hoping for the least bit of information. "I'll get Joe and Manny. They'll be glad you're awake."

Chapter Seven

The limp to the gym seemed longer than normal to Cole. It was the first time he'd taken that hall sober since he was a kid.

Man, he wanted a drink right now. His tongue itched for the burn, and his mind thirsted for the reprieve. He worked to stave off the agitation as if he needed to be alert to any danger. No danger here. At least not the kind that housed insurgents with machine guns, RPGs and cloaked IEDs.

The images of explosions in his brain only gave way to the constant harangue from Joe that he needed a real rehab program. Cole had fought well-trained terrorists. He could resist Johnny Walker.

He wet his lips with his tongue. *Thirsty*.

Today Cole would face Carly for the first time since the hospital. Over the past few days he'd watched her from the window of his suite, walking the grounds, reading a book on the patio. She read for hours at a time. What was in that book?

Thinking back on the dark brown eyes he'd woken to in the hospital, he suddenly wanted to know more about the woman who possessed them. But he'd stayed in his suite from the moment he'd gotten back from the hospital. It was too hard to face anyone in his weakened condition.

Carly.

Her name came to mind more easily these days even if it took a slight delay. Still, he liked the moniker, Beauty, better. He'd loved the self-conscious posture she'd displayed that first day he used it—the humility, endearing. He'd loved the ire it drew, on later dates, causing her brown eyes to burn. But most of all he thought of the smile she'd given him on hearing it in the hospital. He longed to touch her face as her expression registered relief on seeing him conscious—like he was important to her.

Of course he was. His investment in her prosthetics would be prodigious. He needed Jurvis to investigate her, just in case. But why had he kept delaying?

He thumped down the hall, his scalp still smarting from the close shave he'd given his head to rid it of the growth of the past few days, then entered the gym.

Carly stood near the sink and turned. Her eyes grew wide with the gasp. "Cole, you're bleeding." She grabbed a tissue and ran to him. Reaching up, she patted the left side of his bald head. "What happened?"

He took the tissue from her and held it to the spot. "Cut myself shaving."

"That's one nasty cut."

"I had to do a few passes to get it close enough. The scar sometimes gets in the way." And his hands still weren't that steady.

Carly searched through the cabinet and pulled out the first aid kit. "Sit, Cole. Let me put a bandage on it."

He sat on the chair by the sink. She opened a tube of gel and applied some to the wound. He drew in the scent of coconut, thoughts of a rum-filled Pina Colada working through him, and peeked up at her. "Will I live?"

Her face was tense as she smoothed the bandage and opened another tube. Why didn't she answer him? His situation couldn't be that dire. She smoothed some cream around the area, her warm fingers so gentle on his skin. He wondered what the extra cream was for, but didn't dare ask as it might halt her ministrations. Cole closed his eyes and relaxed his muscles. Her fingers trailed the side of his head, a line down his face to his lip. Her voice a whisper. "Who's Beckett?"

Cole grabbed her wrist. "What are you doing?"

Her breath caught.

"What are you putting on my scar?"

Carly showed him the tube. "It's to soften the tissue."

He jerked her hand away. "Who says I want it softened?"

She turned from him and replaced the first-aid items.

"Am I too ugly to work with?"

Her gaze met his. "You're not too ugly, Cole." Her voice firm. "Just too hurt."

He banged his left fist into his thigh, his eye catching the rubbing alcohol bottle on the counter. *Thirsty*. He swallowed bile. "What's that supposed to mean."

"Why do you shave your head every day? To remind us of your disfigurement?"

"You've been talking to Joe too much."

"What is it you want us to know about you? That you're too bad, untouchable, less than whole?"

All of the above. "Can you leave any part of me alone? I thought you came to give me arms and legs, not re-invent me." If he could pace he'd do it now, but his body would not cooperate, so he thumped his crutch and growled, feeling the deep lack of his silver thermos.

Carly knelt in front of him, eyes beseeching his. Her lips tilted in that funny smile of hers. "Your head is so shiny I can almost see my reflection."

He almost laughed at the distorted view of herself she'd have around the awful scar. His muscles released.

"Why must you make your scars the first things people see in you, when there's so much more to know?"

More to know? "That's not my intention."

"But Joe says—"

"Joes thinks he knows everything." In fact, he knew too much. "I just don't like the way the hair puckers around the wound." He shrugged. "It gives me a cowlick."

By the amused look in her eyes, he didn't expect she believed him. Her right hand traveled toward his temple. He closed his eyes at her oh, so gentle touch, his mouth completely dry.

"If you grew your hair a little long, it'd lay down." Her fingers trailed the line. "Longer hair might suit you."

He caught her fingers in his hand and opened his eyes to meet hers. Her shoulders rose and fell on a breath as she withdrew them. Carly gathered the check sockets, liners and fitting stand, placing them near the parallel bars. She picked up the gel liner and touched it to the end of his residual leg. "And if you ever want to tell me about Beckett," she rolled the liner over his thigh, "I'm a good listener."

~*~

The meal started off quiet. Mrs. Rivera served chicken ... and milk. The thought of the white, phlegmy beverage made Cole shudder. How much longer must he abstain? Oh yeah, forever, according to Joe and Carly. A sigh escaped. He couldn't fathom it.

The chicken wasn't as hard to cut as steak, but Mrs. Rivera had cut both of theirs just the same. Still, Carly forked her meat and ate as though she didn't know the housekeeper did it to protect his pride.

Pride in what? Cole had nothing to be proud of. All he owned had been given to him by someone else. He couldn't even be proud of the ones who'd given it to him since they'd received the same from their parents. It had been many generations since the Harrisons had built their empire, and Cole didn't even know what it had been built on. He was only taught how to invest it and enjoy its fruits.

He took a sip of the milk and unstuck his tongue from the roof of his mouth. *Thirsty.*

"Now you're staring at me."

Cole loved the pucker between Carly's brows when she was annoyed. He smirked. "Yes I am."

She dropped her fork. "What are you thinking about?"

His mind ran through ideas, not believing the answer of "you" would go over too well. "I was thinking about how well those sockets fit today—like they were a part of me. You really know your business."

"Remember, those are only the check-sockets, used to help us get the best fit. The real sockets will be made from the shapes we created today."

He sipped his milk again, dreaming of a rum chaser. "It was exciting watching you wield a blow torch." She'd looked so intent on her work, heating the mold and adjusting it accordingly.

Her eyes lit with humor. "Did I scare you?"

"Impressed me." He watched the color rise to her cheeks. "You take a lot of pride in what you do."

Carly shrugged. "It's important to me. My father's dream of helping amputees is a good one."

"Your father's dream." Why did Cole sense something missing? "Is it your dream too?"

"Yes." She drew a stray hair behind her ear. "It's the least I can do for the vets who've sacrificed everything for my country."

Something in her hesitation made Cole wonder if the father-daughter dream of starting a new company was so perfectly matched.

"My father also taught me to do everything as if for God."

"God." The word came from Cole like a curse. Unbidden, thoughts of Beckett flooded his mind.

Thirsty.

Beckett had done things for God too. Carly said she'd like to hear about Beckett. Did she really? Maybe she should know what this God had done to one of His most faithful.

Her gaze searched him. "How are you doing?"

Not this question. She wouldn't like the answer.

"I mean," she twirled the rice around in her dish, "with the ... drinking?" The last word barely audible.

"Are you asking do I crave it?" *Thirsty.*

She pressed her lips, then, "Yes."

His jaw grew ridged. "Every stinkin' second."

Her attention landed in her plate.

He drew a breath. "But that's to be expected."

She swirled the rice around some more. "Can you tell me about it? Combat?" She peeked up. "Maybe it would help to talk about it."

Talk, talk, talk. Why is it everyone thought talk was the cure? "You don't want to hear about war. Believe me."

"I want to hear about whatever you need to tell me."

Why was she being so open, so kind? He'd never been anything but unruly to her.

Her fingers found their way to the cross at her neck as her posture seemed to deflate. "How about Beckett?"

"What do you know about Beckett?"

Thirsty.

He hadn't mentioned Beckett to anyone. Why did she keep saying that name as though it were as meaningful to her as it was to him?

"I only know you scr—I mean—said his name in the hospital and that every time I mention him, something unfathomable passes through your eyes."

Curse that Joe, letting her near as Cole thrashed like a wild animal, deep in his hallucinations. Why had Joe allowed her to see him so weak?

Her gaze met his. "Like now."

"Like now, what?"

"Your eyes. They're intense. Something about Beckett causes you pain."

Thirsty.

He swiped at his chin with the linen napkin from his lap and moved to stand. Carly reached toward him. "Please, Cole. Tell me." She grabbed the cross again. "Something tells me you need to speak."

Did he?

He sat.

"Fine." He'd tell her how this God of hers failed His most faithful human.

~*~

He said "fine," but sat in silence. Was that an agreement to tell her or something else? Carly remained quiet, knowing he needed time to process and move at his own pace. She'd worked with veterans before. Many very bitter. Many emotionally scarred. She knew God could heal all wounds, but didn't know how to get the soldiers to accept Him or what it looked like when they did. Only that God could heal anything.

Couldn't He?

"Beckett joined my platoon fresh out of Basic." He shook his head, eyelids falling in a heavy blink. "He'd come to Basic straight from high school. Still had all the pimples to prove it."

Carly tried not to stare at the raw emotion displayed in Cole's features. His left hand fiddling with the linen napkin.

"He was eager to kill the enemy. Too eager." Cole's laugh was bitter. "Save his country from the evil-doers and all that." He shook his head. "I didn't look forward to the first time he actually did. I knew it would change him. He cared too much about each person he met. All my men joked about it. Even bet on how he'd react at his first kill—cry, vomit, go psycho or AWOL. But secretly, we were all afraid for him."

"I pushed him hard—harder than anyone else. Part of my mind told me it was to make him tough, but the other part was hoping he'd beg to be transferred. Not likely in war, but still."

Cole looked up from the napkin. "Do you know what he said, one day after I'd drilled him especially hard?" His blues eyes sought the question more than his words.

Carly could barely speak looking into them. "What?"

"He said, 'Thank you, sir.' I asked, 'For what?' and he said, 'For making me a better Marine.'" Cole's shoulders rose and dropped at the breath forced out. He scoffed. "A better Marine. I just wanted him gone."

Cole waited as the grandfather clock finished seven gongs. "Then the day finally came. We were in a street fight in Ramadi. We were hours behind buildings shooting at snipers on roof tops and around corners. My men were well trained so we picked off our share of the enemy. Just what Beckett said he'd wanted to do. He took one off the roof. The guy fell to the street and lay there in a tangled heap, blood everywhere. I eyed Beckett, prepared to deal with the potential impact. I could see his Adam's apple bob as he swallowed hard at the image. Beckett's chin quivered, but his sight never wavered. He picked off two more enemy on the dirt road."

Was Cole proud of the young Marine, or embarrassed he'd been wrong? Carly couldn't figure out how this event had traumatized this man to the point his eyes raged whenever Beckett's name was mentioned. She could tell there was more, so she let silence give him permission to continue.

"When we got back to camp, he'd disappeared. Several of the men joked he'd gone AWOL. I looked everywhere and when I couldn't find him I started to panic, wondering if it was true. Finally, I checked the make-shift chapel and there he sat. His agonizing sobs made it hard for me to near, but I knew I needed to. He sat, face in his palms, black-leather book open on his lap. I could tell he'd noticed me, but he didn't stop crying, so I waited."

"Finally, a broken voice emerged. 'How do you do it, sir?' he said. I assumed he meant the killing, but I didn't have an answer so I gave him none. I'd figured it had something to do with never getting close, unlike Beckett, who'd learned the local's names and gave candy to the children. Still, it didn't seem the proper time to reprimand him for that."

"The sobs quieted, his chest labored up and down with his hard breaths. His finger ran along some words on the book in front of him and he seemed to calm. I couldn't see the type on the page, just the title on the top—Psalms. He later told me he read those because they were written by a warrior king, someone who knew the horrors of war, but could also pray for those who persecuted him. I never got that, but I wasn't going to question him on it either. I just know it seemed to help after a fight and I was good with that."

The way the chandelier's light swam in the liquid of Cole's eyes brought a lump to Carly's throat. He must have sensed it because he dropped his gaze to the table and fisted the linen napkin.

"I left the chapel, but watched for him. He came out an hour later. In the weeks that followed, I found him on his knees at every break." Cole's lip curled. "I guess he was beseeching his God." The way Cole's finger circled the rim of his milk glass, Carly knew he wished it filled with liquor. "Like this God would save him." The venom in Cole's voice burned. "Still, Becket didn't crack, he got stronger. We all expected him to stop learning the language from the locals and giving stuff to the kids, but he didn't. In fact, he seemed more intent to treat them as friends."

Carly's eyes stung with forming tears. By the look on Cole's face she suspected the end of the story would be tragic, but she wouldn't find out tonight because Cole pushed himself up with his crutch and hobbled out of the dining room. "I need some air."

She watched him shrink in the distance of the hallway, wishing she could meet the man who'd inspired such emotion in Cole, but she suspected that would be impossible this side of heaven.

Chapter Eight

"Hey, Carly." Manny waved before he shot the basketball into the hoop mounted to the side of the garage. Carly waved back and smiled at the young man in blue jeans that dragged the concrete over his bare feet.

"Nice shot." Cole focused on Manny without even turning to greet Carly himself. "Now let's see you do it one-handed."

"Show me again." Manny tossed him the ball as if careful to aim it toward the intact hand. Cole curled his arm around it to catch, rolled the ball on his chest to position it in his palm, then lobbed it at the basket. Their easy banter lent the idea that this was not a first time event and wouldn't be a last.

Carly wasn't close enough to hear the rest of the conversation as she headed toward the stables. The image conjured the tale of the young Marine Cole had spoken of the night before. Her heart ached at the pain she'd seen, so evident in is his blue eyes. What was the rest of that story? Would he ever tell her? She wanted to know more about the softer side of this man she lived with, but he seemed most protective of it.

Carly quickened her steps to the stable, needing to speak with the hippotherapist before Cole joined them. The weathered wooden building took on an ominous gloom, its enlarging figure threatening to engulf Carly as she neared. A horse whinnied sending lightning down her back. Ha! Lightning. That horse was certainly the origin of her panic. She halted and steadied her breath. Did Joe really expect her to walk beside that enormous animal? What could she do? Catch Cole if he fell? Not likely.

She heard the clip-clop of hooves even before the man appeared leading Lightning out of the stables. His softened Asian features almost mirrored those of Joe's, though more westernized and younger. His worn jeans and NEEDTOBREATHE concert T told Carly she'd like the man. Relaxed, and had great taste in music.

He caught her eye. "You must be Carly." The warmth in his expression brought a measure of comfort.

But only a measure.

She stood at a distance, eying the large, dark monster beside him. "Yes."

"I'm Sam. Joe's son." He reached out to shake, but when Carly hesitated, he stepped away from the animal to grasp her hand. His smile grew into the same shape Joe's did as he looked between her and Lightning. He patted the horse's neck. "You a little nervous?"

She chuckled. "How'd you guess? The sweat on my brow? My trembling hands? Or the oceans of distance I like to keep between me and him ... uh ... her?"

"None of the above. Dad told me."

"Guess I didn't hide it very well."

"Hide something from my father?" He grimaced. "Not likely."

Carly scanned the pasture by the stable. "Look, is this really necessary, getting Cole to ride today?" She shoved her hands in her jeans pockets. "He doesn't even have the prosthetics yet. Shouldn't we wait until he's accustomed to them before he starts?"

Sam's eyes sparked, his smile grew. "Not to mention it might be dangerous for you."

Carly harrumphed.

Sam stroked the mane of the beast. "Dad said we better get him on before he changes his mind. He and Lightning have a history together. Once Cole rides, they'll likely fall into it again."

She sucked in a breath. "It's the 'fall into' part that worries me. They have a history for that as well."

Sam's fingers ran the length of Lightning's nose. He shook his head. "That won't happen this time. Lightning is too old for that kind of speed anymore. Which is what makes her perfect for this job. Most therapy horses are retired. Besides, we won't let them go too fast."

"I still don't like it."

"Carly, this is more than getting a man on a horse. This is both physical therapy and even psychotherapy for him. We're using horses to help wounded vets heal from physical trauma, brain injury and even PTSD." He drew in a breath as if knowing he'd need sustenance against her negativity. "At the very least it will help teach him how to walk with two legs again."

How could a horse teach Cole how to walk? Wasn't that her job? "I can do that fine, as his physical therapist, and without a horse."

He sighed. "I'm sure you can, but this can only add to what you're doing." He looked at the horse with endearment. "And while it does, he'll enjoy it. Riding a horse simulates the back and forth motion of walking in the hips." He pointed to the striped blanket over the horse's back. "When doing therapy, we don't use a saddle. That way, the rider feels the motion without needing to exert the effort himself. It becomes natural. And from what my dad tells me, Mr. Cole's gait is anything but natural. Using the crutch has developed the upper left side of his body and the lower right side in such a way his musculature is uneven. Riding could help to balance him with very little effort on his part."

He stepped the horse closer.

Carly backed away.

Sam's smile tilted. "You'll see. This horse will help Mr. Cole. I'm certain." His eyes grew soft. "I remember watching him ride when I was a boy." He shook his head as if words couldn't describe the image. "They were amazing together. Like one. There's a bond between horse and rider, even when they don't have the history these two had. Patients who have difficulty in relationships, for whatever reason, can have one better with a horse. And relationships heal."

Carly folded her arms, but something about that last statement resonated. Yes, Carly knew her own work was about more than providing adaptive equipment. She'd miss that piece sitting in the business office of the company her dad wanted her to start.

Sam wiggled his brows. "Who knows, we might even get you to bond with Lightning."

Now that was crazy. "To think, I was almost beginning to find you credible," she said on a laugh.

Cole appeared on the path, hobbling up the hill with his lone crutch. He took in the occupational therapist, then swung his attention to Carly. His jaw tensed.

Lightning whinnied and shook her mane as he neared, her hooves moved restlessly beneath her as though trying to get to something she loved. Cole's attention moved to the horse. He stopped and stared, his chest rising and falling in long, slow waves. His gaze seemed to absorb the animal as though finally reunited with something long ago treasured.

His expression seemed to tangle with emotion until he spied Carly, arms folded more tightly around her as she stepped away from the agitated creature.

His left brow rose. "You okay, Beauty?"

She rubbed her upper arms. "I'm fine."

Cole's lips lifted into a sardonic grin.

"Mr. Cole, I'm Sam, Joe's son."

Cole scanned the man up and down. "Yes," he drawled. "You've grown since I last saw you."

Sam hesitated. "Um ... well ... It's been about fifteen years."

Cole neared Lightning and smoothed her mane. She whinnied at his touch, her tail swishing back and forth. "So you're an occupational therapist now?"

"Yes, for several years."

Cole fingered the blanket over the horse's back and turned to stare down at Sam. "Where do we start?"

Sam led the horse to a ramped platform. "Dad built this so you could mount the horse more easily."

Cole hobbled up the incline.

Sam held the reins to keep the horse still. "Carly, why don't you help him with his crutch."

Carly stepped on the platform, took the crutch and allowed Cole to use her shoulder for support as he swung his residual left leg over the horse. Lightning stood absolutely still as if she knew the importance of this ride.

"Now, Carly, come along to the side and walk with Lightning."

She hesitated, stepped down the ramp and neared as the horse began to move forward.

Cole chuckled. "Is she supposed to catch me from falling—way over there?"

Sam laughed.

Carly inched closer, but kept enough distance not to get stepped on. Her body tensed at full alert to every move the beast might make.

But there was a stillness in the air as the horse's hooves landed in the grass in a calming, four-part rhythm. Carly could almost feel the movement between man and beast, in tandem with each other. Cole sat high on Lightning's back, as though perched on a throne. A bird sang from a tree. The wind rustled through Carly's hair bringing the mingled scent of both pine and horseflesh to her nostrils, but none of that drowned out the sound of the grass.

Until she heard Cole's breath become labored.

Sam didn't give any instruction, just walked along the pasture, allowing the movement to rock Cole's body side to side and front to back. Carly's muscles relaxed as she sensed the care of the animal for her master.

Cole's labored breathing hitched and Carly worried he may be having a relapse of the DTs or a flashback of combat. She stole a glance to find his expression fighting emotion that struggled to be set free. He looked away. Carly dropped her gaze to the animal's shoulder, watching its muscles contract and release, push and pull.

Another hitch from his vocal chords as his left hand slid round the neck of the animal and held fast. Cole buried his face in Lightning's mane; an agonizing sob rent the air. It wrung Carly's heart dry. She could hardly breathe.

Sam stilled the horse. Carly neared, worrying Cole might fall. He'd latched on, practically prostate over Lightning's absolutely silent form. Carly placed a hand over Cole's. He grasped her fingers as more sobs shook his body, muffled into the sleek shiny coat of his friend.

What could she do now? She looked to Sam for clues. He stood, motionless as though this was not unexpected. He nodded to Carly, which told her not to worry—and that he was right.

Moments seemed to turn to hours before a great sniffling sound emerged and Cole wiped his eyes on the horse's mane. He drew in a sustaining breath, sat straight and commanded in a strangled voice, "Walk on."

The horse moved forward, Cole sitting straight again, Carly's hand still in his. It was at that point Carly realized, she was right up against the horse ... and it didn't bother her one bit.

~*~

Carly shifted left in her bed, then right. Tangled in her sheets, she bolted up. Sleep would not come, only thoughts of the past several weeks. Fitting Cole with the prosthetics and beginning his rehab brought so many emotions to the surface. She'd expected Cole to be emotional—as often happens when a patient walks again after a period of disability—but the most intense soul-stirring had been *hers*.

Her mind had replayed Cole's first ride with Lightning as she'd warned him the initial prosthetic alignment appointments often caused some vulnerability for patients.

He stood on the new limb, leaning heavily on the parallel bars, his gaze catching her with his droll expression. "Do you expect me to cry?"

She didn't know how to respond, feeling as though she'd intruded on an intimate moment between the man and his horse the day before. He almost seemed to be challenging her to bring it up.

She didn't dare.

His gaze dropped to the new foot, lathering his words with the arrogance only he could bestow, "I promise I'll maintain better control of myself today."

And he did. Except for a few moments where his voice had cracked.

He kept telling her the new leg felt good, when she could see in his gait it was not. She'd adjust the prosthesis more, and his breath would catch at the change. "This is much better than the leg I had before." He walked back and forth, brow in a knot, breaths coming in excited waves. He looked at Carly like a little boy on Christmas day with a present he didn't know he wanted. Her heart swelled and broke at the same time.

The past several weeks of rehab brought more of the same. That's what kept her awake at two o'clock in the morning. The idea that a human being would settle for less in his life, his body, and his relationships, because he believed nothing better existed.

Cole, there is so much more.

It seemed the only cure for the roller coaster of her mind would be to get one of Mrs. Rivera's lemon bars from the kitchen. Maybe a heavy dose of carbohydrates would soothe her troubled nerves.

Carly took the long walk through the upstairs hall, past all those rooms that were built to be filled with party guests. She padded down the stairs, pulling her terry robe tighter around her PJs, clutching her light romance read in her hand. The novel should help take her mind off the heaviness that was Cole's empty world.

She could almost taste the tart lemon bars now.

"No!" Cole's voice pierced the quiet.

Carly's attention jerked toward the hall to his room.

"*Get down-get down-get down.*" The words shot like a rapid-fire machine-gun.

She ran to his opened bedroom door and found him wrestling his sheets. Who was he fighting and how would it end? Carly froze.

She couldn't just stand there, but what could she do?

Cole's body calmed, but his breaths still labored. Carly neared his bed, clutching her novel, and watched.

"Move!" More an order than a shout.

That day in the hospital her touch seemed to soothe him. Should she try again? She knelt to his side and laid her book on the floor. His body jerked and she fell back.

Carly approached again, Cole's breaths heaving in large gulps. Should she touch his hand? What would he do if he woke to find her there?

She pulled back, but felt the need to stop the nightmare, so she reached out again, her hand meeting his.

Cole rolled onto Carly and thrust her to the floor. She flailed against his weight. He shoved his residual forearm into her chin, squeezing her windpipe.

She worked to form words against the crush of her vocal chords. His eyes were open but dark and hollow. Carly could almost see into hell.

"Cole," she choked. Carly thrashed some more, wriggling from his grip. "Cole!"

He jerked, eyes sparking to life. His expression ran waves of disgust, pain then horror in one eternal second. He rolled off her. "What are you doing here?" His voice like flint on rock.

Carly filled her lungs with the air she'd been denied. Her mind screeched to a halt, grateful her life still resided within her. She reached to her neck, caressing the skin just in his death grip. "You were …" she pulled in a breath, " … having a …" another breath, " … nightmare."

"And you appointed yourself my savior?"

His anger startled her. "No." What could she say? "I … it just looked horrible."

His expression confirmed it had been. "What were you doing in my room?"

She sat up. "I heard you scream."

He turned his body to lift himself off the floor. "Well, don't worry about me. I can take care of myself."

She stood and closed her bathrobe around her. "I'm sorry. I didn't mean to intrude." She strode out the door and bypassed the main kitchen. Not even Mrs. Rivera's lemon bars could assuage her mind now. She'd need to spend time in face-on-the-floor kind of prayer. Cole's needs were too great for any one person to bear. Joe was right. There was only One who could help this man.

Chapter Nine

Carly couldn't believe she found herself heading toward the stable this morning for a measure of peace. This place usually made her tremble in fear. But Joe's gentle wisdom always poured over her like a warm shower. She needed that after last night's run-in with Cole.

Joe brushed the length of a dapple grey, smaller than the beast Cole liked to ride. His eyes twinkled as he greeted her. "You know this is where we keep the horses, don't you?"

She smirked back. "Yes, Joe, I do."

"Sam tells me you and Lightning are getting along better these days."

"We've closed the distance." She didn't mention how much she enjoyed watching Cole trot on the large animal, no longer needing her at his side.

Joe clapped dust off his hands. "That's great. Maybe we'll get you to ride Miss Gray, here, before long." He patted the horse. She whinnied.

"Ha! Don't press your luck, Mr. Sakamoto."

He pushed the brush deep into the grooves around the horse's flank. "So what brings you to the stable?"

Carly's hand found the skin at her neck, still raw from the night before. "Cole has terrible nightmares."

Joe's expression sobered as his gaze traveled to her fingers. "Did he do that to you?"

"He didn't mean to." She shook her head. "I don't think he was even awake. His eyes were so …" a chill ran through her at the memory, " … vacant."

Joe stopped brushing. "It's the PTSD. Sometimes Cole has flashbacks during the day." Joe dropped onto a stool. "A few months ago he yelled at Manny to keep a distance from the trash truck driving in front of them." He shook his head. "Because it could be loaded with insurgents. Manny said he'd glanced in the rearview afterward and Cole looked totally embarrassed—like he'd just realized what he'd said. He's always on high-alert."

"Can anything be done for him?"

Joe sucked in a sustaining breath. "Sure, if only he'd acknowledge he needs help and accepts it. Unfortunately our boy is filled with a lethal dose of pride."

Carly thought about the number of vets she'd rehabbed. "I wonder what makes one soldier more prone to PTSD than others."

"Who knows? All sorts of soldiers, from wonderful families, struggle with it. But I'd guess it doesn't help that Cole has never asked for help. I fear he believes no one really cares. And it's hard to understand the ugliness of war without relying on the sovereignty of an eternal God who can turn even that into something good."

Carly's eyes burned. "I'm not even sure I, with all my years in church, can do that."

Joe's smile warmed her. "That doesn't come from sitting on a pew, but lots and lots of time with your Savior and plenty of personal struggles cleansed by the Lord."

"Yeah, I guess so."

"Cole is a man with many demons, Carly. He entered the Marines for all the wrong reasons. Now, he's left with flashbacks, hyper-vigilance, and without limbs or a reason to live."

He hitched his thumb in his belt loop. "A man needs purpose, and Cole feels none."

The tear ran warm down Carly's cheek. Joe's gaze seemed to follow it. She swiped it away, completely powerless against this challenge.

Joe's brows narrowed. "Are you …?" He shook his head. "Never mind."

What was he going to ask? And why did Carly suddenly feel exposed? She looked at Joe one final time before turning to leave. He nodded his goodbye. She prayed all the way back to the house. It was all she could do.

~*~

Cole nursed the Dr. Pepper in the living room, wishing with all he had it packed more power. His nerves buzzed and jolted at every sound. Poor Mrs. Rivera tip-toed through the kitchen, so as not to receive any more of Cole's rage.

Did she have to drop that pan an hour ago? He'd reached for his gun, but found none. Of course not. He no longer carried. In fact, he'd found no real finger to pull the trigger, either. Only the myo-electric arm he'd been struggling to master over the past several weeks. But the instinct to defend himself was there just the same.

Just one sip of—Oh, he didn't care what. He'd take kerosene right now. Even the rubbing alcohol and mouthwash in the bathroom medicine cabinet called his name. But he'd resisted ... for now.

The front door clicked open. Footsteps, then Charles Jurvis, the Harrison family's long-time man-of-business, appeared in the living-room archway. "Sheesh, Cole. You look awful."

Cole ran his parched tongue along the back of his teeth. *Thirsty.*

Of course he looked awful in contrast to Jurvis's crisp, pin-striped suit. Sunlight glowed through the window from behind him, casting a halo that framed his close-cropped, graying afro and ebony features.

Cole had always liked Jurvis, who seemed a Wall Street prophet. He had a wisdom about the financial world. Probably a mixture of genius and what he picked up trailing his mother as a boy when she cleaned the house of a wealthy investor.

Cole dropped the paperback novel he'd been flipping through on the end table. Drivel. He couldn't imagine who'd read that romance stuff—smoldering eyes and heaving breasts.

Jurvis eyed it. "Your taste in reading has changed since last I visited."

Cole shook his head. "That's Carly's."

"The girl you wanted me to investigate?"

"It's her family I wanted you to investigate."

"Same difference." Jurvis opened the cabinets beneath the wet bar.

"She left it in my bedroom last night."

Jurvis turned, eyes wide. "Am I too late?"

Cole scrubbed his face. "She heard one of my nightmares and came to help."

"Uh-oh. She plays the caring type. It seems I am too late." He opened another empty cabinet.

"You won't find anything in there."

Jurvis pivoted, glass in hand. "Why not?"

"We cleared the house of alcohol." He blinked. "It seems I'm to be sober now." Cole's tongue trailed the roof of his over-dry mouth.

Jurvis's gaze lingered on the glass. "Ah, that explains your eyes darting around in your head, your agitated appearance," he pointed. "And I think you missed a spot shaving your head today."

Cole's hand absently reached to his scar before he caught the joke in his lawyer's eyes. "So what have you found?"

Jurvis rummaged the mini-fridge for a Coke and poured it into his tumbler. "Nothing really." He took a seat in front of Cole. "At least not more than we already knew. The company's being sued. The prosthetics are defective." He gestured to the arm and leg Cole wore as a matter of course these days. "Why in the world would you try their products?"

"Don't knock them. Look. I can now do the key grip." Cole raised his myo-electric arm, rolled the metal digits in and closed the thumb on the side of the pointer finger. It took an eternity, but he'd finally gotten the dynamics down. "Here's the power grip." He moved the thumb manually with his left hand, then worked his arm muscles to close his fingers with the thumb over the middle digits. "And how about the mouse grip." Cole worked again to close the thumb and pinky with the other fingers straighter. He maneuvered his arm as though moving a computer mouse.

Jurvis's eyebrows rose in mock salute. "Impressive. Now if only you could do the martini grip to hand me a drink, I'd be thrilled."

Cole would have to practice that one—not. He sighed.

"Bet you can't do this." Cole worked his muscles to command the hand to spin a 360 on its wrist. He loved that ability. It reminded him of a toy car he'd gotten as a kid that twirled on the floor.

At the glazing of Jurvis's eyes, Cole stilled the hand and got back to business. "How about the father? What did you find out about the company when he ran it?"

Jurvis shrugged. "Top notch as far as I can tell. Many of the older physical therapists I spoke with said they were the most recommended a decade ago."

"So what Henry told me was true?"

Jurvis crossed one long leg over the other. "It may have been true, but who's to say the daughter isn't more like the sons than she is the father."

"I don't think so."

Jurvis folded his arms over his chest. "Don't you think you should have researched her before you let her move in and sober you?" His smile edged up one side. " … come to your bedroom at night and give you body parts?"

Cole tensed. Why did he feel the need to protect Carly's honor? "It's not like that."

"Than what is it like?"

"I trust her father. He seemed to be someone who really cared about what he was doing." Something about his attention to Cole on the walk home in the snow, and his eyes as he told the story of his brother. "I wanted to do this for him."

Jurvis sipped his un-doctored soda and winced. "Well let's just hope they aren't playing you for an overly wealthy fool."

"Cole, I thought we'd—" Carly halted in the archway.

Jurvis stood and held out his hand. "You must be Ms. Rose."

She shook it.

"I've heard so much about you."

Carly turned to look at Cole.

"This is Charles Jurvis, Carly. My lawyer."

"Oh. Nice to meet you."

Cole held the romance novel out to her, using his myo-electric arm. "I believe this is yours."

She smiled like a proud teacher and neared to recover it. She tugged. "Now you need to let go."

"Oh, right." He worked his arm muscles and the metal fingers opened.

"Where'd you find this? I've been looking for it everywhere."

"You left it in my bedroom last night."

Cole loved the way her cheeks pinked as she glanced self-consciously at Jurvis. Jurvis's smile only added to her color. There was something so innocent about her. It drew Cole in. Jurvis would call it a wolf in sheep's clothing. Cole hoped she was just a sheep.

What are you really, Beauty?

She clutched the novel against her ribs. "I expected you in the gym ten minutes ago."

"Oh, I'm sorry." His hippocampus must be on strike again today. "Jurvis came and I completely forgot."

Jurvis drained his glass and thumped it on the bar. "That's okay. I'm leaving." He glanced at Carly. "Nice to meet you Ms. Rose." He strolled out the door.

"I didn't mean to send him away."

"We were done anyway."

"It's just that you've been doing so well with the leg, I wanted to suggest we prepare you for a hike. We'll work on maneuvering the knee to bend more fluidly, and strengthen your muscles. We can even try out that other foot I told you about that's good on rough terrain." She looked excited about the possibilities. "Then you can show me the spot you've mentioned. You know, the one where you saw my father."

Henry, the man Cole now realized had saved him from ending his own life. Was Carly more like her father or her brothers? Cole wished he could know for sure.

Chapter Ten

There she sat. Reading that confounded romance novel at the patio table. Cole would never have expected her to be the type to read that stuff. He closed the French doors with a thud and she jolted. Must have been pretty engrossed.

"Oh. Cole. You're here." She placed the paperback on the table. "You ready for the hike?"

He caught the heel of his prosthetic leg on the step in order to hinge it to bend. "Yup."

Her brown eyes softened as she watched him maneuver. "Is that the hiking foot?"

"Mm-hm." He patted his leg. "Let's test drive this baby."

She lifted the metal crutch from the chair beside her.

Cole shook his head. "I don't need a crutch."

Carly smirked. "I knew you'd say that. That's why I got it myself. It's for safety while you get used to the terrain with a new limb. You know, normal people sometimes use a walking stick on a hike."

He harrumphed as he received it from her outstretched grasp and led the way to the woods. "Are you suggesting I'm not normal?"

She remained close beside him. "No. Only that it's okay for you to be human every now and again."

They entered the forested path. Carly's eyes sparkled as her gaze swept the trees overhead. She drew in a deep breath. "I love the smell here. It's intoxicating."

He couldn't help but smile. At the moment, Cole was intoxicated himself.

He stumbled when the leg didn't bend quickly, then caught himself with the crutch. Carly's eyes met his with an I-told-you-so smile, but she said not a word. He smirked back. It was amazing how much they communicated in silence these days. Like they knew each other so well. In fact, no one on earth seemed to know all his flaws as she did. And yet, she didn't run in the other direction. Of course, his staff had stayed for years, but they were paid well to do so. Carly must want his investment in her new designs something fierce. He couldn't think of any other reason she'd endure so much.

He gestured for her to lead the way, pointing the correct path at the fork. He wanted to watch the wonder on her face. It seemed to mirror his own pleasure as he traveled these woods. She'd call it God's creation. Cole couldn't understand how a God could make the beauty of the trees, the flowers, the songs of the birds, the fresh smell of the earth below, and still allow the ugliness of war. He chose not to believe at all.

He couldn't wait to show Carly his perch.

"So." His voice held a bit of mischief. "Tell me of this literary tome you're reading."

Did she just turn pink? "What literary tome?"

"Your novel. The one you can't seem to get enough of. It must be very good."

She smiled, almost sheepishly. "It is."

"What's it about?"

"It's a romance." She dropped her gaze to the uneven terrain. "Watch out here."

Cole maneuvered, working to hinge the leg and balancing with the crutch. "Is that all? No story. Just romance."

"Oh yes, there's a story, but I read it more for the relationship between the man and the woman. This writer really knows how to draw you into their lives. I love it."

"Hmmmm."

"I see you don't approve."

"It's not my job to approve or disapprove of what you read. You just always struck me as the classics type."

She turned to Cole. "Oh, I am. But that doesn't mean I can't enjoy something contemporary— something I can relate to, and yet will allow me to escape from the stress of the day."

He dropped his gaze to the prosthetic foot teetering over a rock, his mind assaulted by all she'd witnessed of his unseemly life. "I guess, um, you could use an escape."

She stopped and turned. Her brow crunched as she considered him then held out her hand.

"I've got it." The ground wasn't that difficult.

"Cole you can ask for help if you need it."

"I don't need it." They walked on.

"Escape, now and then, is good." Her whispered words hung in the air. "What my brothers have done to my father's company weighs on me. It's bad enough they didn't take their customer's needs seriously, but ruining my father's dream—their father's dream—really cuts deep. My father wasn't the most present man to his family while building his company, but he never deserved that kind of betrayal."

The leaves under their feet crunched and the branches snapped as they treaded the path. Cole loved the sounds. It reminded him of the goal, the journey to his domain. It filled him with awe and wonder at the forces that created it. Whatever those forces might be.

"So tell me this story that helps you escape from your brothers' evil dealings."

"It's about a woman who inherited a ranch in Montana and falls in love with the foreman who runs it."

"Ah. That's why the man with the bulging muscles on the cover wears a cowboy hat."

She giggled. "Yup."

"The cowboy hat gets 'em every time."

She pinked again.

"Of course the bulging muscles never hurt." He pointed to a path with a slight incline.

Her gaze seemed to drop to his biceps as he worked the crutch to steady himself. "Guess not."

Cole grunted.

"They don't always need bulging muscles." Her smile held a magic to it. "They just need to be willing to slay the dragon."

He raised a brow. "There's a dragon in Montana?"

Carly chuckled. "Not really a dragon. In every good romance the man needs to be willing to risk something to get the heroine what she needs."

He watched his one foot, then his high-tech foot, alternate in view as he trudged the path. "I guess I'd never make a good hero in a romance novel."

She stopped and turned to him. Something in her eyes pierced him, but she remained silent as if she were fighting what to say. She chose to say nothing and turned back to the path.

"Take that hill." He pointed to the root-covered sloped wall.

"You call that a hill?" Carly surveyed the dirt, grass and rocks that led up to his perch. "That's a climb. You didn't tell me there'd be a climb."

"You didn't ask. Besides, it's not that steep."

"We can't do that. You're not ready."

"I climbed that hill before I had the prosthetics. I can do it now."

"You were used to climbing without. Using them is a whole different type of work."

"Then I'll take them off." Cole gestured to the knotted dirt. "We're going up that hill."

Carly scanned his features. Cole made sure what she saw in them meant business. Evidently, it did.

"Fine. But be careful and do what I say."

"Aren't you the bossy one?"

She thrust her hands to her hips. "Make sure you lift with the intact limbs and stabilize only, with the prosthetics. That arm was not made to hold an entire body on a climb."

He saluted with the myo-electric limb. It buzzed as he straightened the fingers. "Yes, ma'am."

Cole grabbed hold of an embedded root with his left hand, crutch dangling from his forearm, and stepped into another with his right foot. He swung up as he always did, and steadied himself with the other limbs. They banged into the dirt—not being used to the extra length. He skidded down a few inches.

Carly gasped.

"I'm okay, Beauty." He didn't want her having a heart attack.

A shuffling sounded behind him. "Just be careful, Cole."

He grasped another root and pulled, this time with a better stabilization from the prosthetics. Carly was right. This would take some getting used to. Her breaths hitched at each movement he made.

He called down. "You comin' or not?"

The shuffling sounded again, her voice right beneath him. "I'm coming."

Cole reached the top, and grasped the metal crutch, thrust it into the ground and pulled himself to standing. He headed toward the edge as he heard Carly's labored breaths behind him, and scanned the forest below, following the bird that flew from one tree branch to another, leaving the former to bounce in its wake. A squirrel scurried up a tree and stopped to rub its front paws together. The green of the forest below was so lush he could almost feel it on his skin. And the air. Nothing sweeter than the scent of pine that whistled in the breeze.

"It's beautiful." The awe in Carly's voice washed over him and into him.

He turned to her, his gaze falling into the depth of the brown in her eyes. Like a pit he could never extricate himself from. "What dragon do you need slayed, Beauty?"

Her mouth opened. "What ... what do you mean?"

Did the idea scare her?

"What do you need that might require a hero's risk?"

She turned. "Nothing."

He reached out, tugging her arm, and turned her back. Why did that question bother her? "I see. You can know all my vulnerabilities, but I'm not allowed to know yours. That's not fair, Beauty. Are you saying you are without need from another human being?"

Her gaze dropped.

He wouldn't let her go without the answer. "What dragon do you need slayed?"

Carly peeked up into his eyes as if uncertain how to continue. "My dragon has already been run through."

Cole let go. Why did it feel like someone had punched him in the gut? "I see." He scanned the forest valley that usually brought him so much joy. "I didn't realize you ... I didn't know you had a hero in your life."

She shook her head. "You misunderstand. I only meant that the one thing most important to me, the thing I needed resolved, has been taken care of."

Cole stared, wishing she'd continue, but she seemed most elusive. This made him more curious. "And what was that?"

Carly shot him a fierce look, then turned away.

"Tell me. Please."

She pointed to a tree below. "Is that where my father crashed?"

He nodded, but continued to stare as if to tell her he hadn't let his question go.

Carly turned back, her face uncertain. "You probably realize my father didn't crash his car in these woods on accident. He meant to die that night." Her gaze traveled back to the tree at the bottom of the slope, which still bore the marks of Henry's car. "He was so distraught. Not only was his company in shambles, but his sons were the authors of that destruction."

Where was she going with this story? Yes, Cole had suspected her father's intention. Is this the dragon she was referring to? Then who—?

"I'd been worried about him for months. I watched him like a hawk, offering to go everywhere with him, fearing he'd do something rash." Her voice cracked as she struggled to continue. "I couldn't be there with him that night because of the storm." Carly hesitated. What made this story so hard for her to tell?

"Since the crash," she looked at Cole, "since he met you ... he's been a different person." Her eyes dug into his soul. "I know you hated the idea of using prosthetics again, but you did—for him. You gave him hope. Hope he hadn't had for almost a year."

Cole stared at her an eternal moment before he could form any thoughts, let alone words. "Are you saying that I—"

She sniffed hard and pivoted. "Let's get back. Mrs. Rivera will worry if we're not home for dinner."

~*~

Carly must be nuts. She left Cole standing there with his mouth wide open, his eyes burning with incredulity. She scrambled down the rooted incline. Cole followed, but she hadn't looked back until it dawned on her he might need some help coming down. She hurried to the bottom and turned.

Cole slid judiciously down the slope on his rear end.

"Careful. Your prosthesis is going to catch that—"

It did. He lurched forward and landed on Carly, throwing her to the ground.

"—root." She looked into his eyes, which were inches above hers. His warm breath fell across her cheek.

He pulled up from her chest leaning heavily on his intact hand, his gaze rolling over her face as a smile slid across one side of his. "You okay, Beauty?"

"Mm-hm. You can get off me now."

He hovered. "I don't know."

"Is something wrong? Are you hurt?"

"No." His expression was pensive. "I'm just thinking about our predicament here."

"What predicament?" Should she push him off?

"It kind of reminds me of those scenes in chick flicks."

"You watch chick flicks?"

"Only when no football games are on." He tilted his head. "Anyway, I've noticed—I mean other than the dragon-slaying thing—romances often have times like these where the hero and heroine find themselves in close proximity and the audience wonders if they're going to kiss." His gaze dropped to her lips.

Carly's heart sped. Had she revealed herself too much too soon? Cole had so much baggage she knew she couldn't carry it for him. But on the other hand, she was falling for the caring man imprisoned inside the hard shell.

His blue eyes searched her again. His jaw hardened. "I'm sorry." He pushed up, but Carly held him still.

"They never kiss at first ... in a movie." She met his gaze. "It's too soon. They need more time."

He lifted himself with his crutch. "Ah, yes. I guess I need to study the genre more." He hobbled down the path toward the house. A chipmunk scurried across between them.

Carly watched the animal climb a tree then followed in Cole's wake all the way to the manor.

Chapter Eleven

Cole slammed the patio door behind him and tossed the crutch onto a living room chair, knowing Carly would soon follow.

What a fool. He'd put himself out there, just that little bit—a first since he'd come back disfigured. Of course, she'd reject him. He passed the mirror over the fireplace and caught his reflection. The angry scar squawked at him like a black crow devouring a carcass on a war-torn city street. These were the scars Carly had wanted to soften, to hide in his hair line. And yet, Cole knew, they were a warning to the innocent of the broken man inside.

His gaze drifted to the wet bar across the living room—empty.

What bothered Cole most was that Carly wasn't the type to get hung up on looks. She must despise the man he was—the bitter vet with flashbacks and nightmares. The man who couldn't even get his parents to love him. The man who led the young to their deaths. The man who at this very minute, craved a drink with the same ferocity his lungs craved air.

The patio door clicked opened behind him, ushering in the scent of Carly's coconut lotion. He strode in the other direction.

"Mr. Cole." Mrs. Rivera stepped out of the kitchen. "A package came for you while you were out."

He grasped the manila envelope from Mrs. Rivera as he heard Carly's footsteps patter up the stairway, then headed toward his bedroom and opened the door. Only then did he notice the name of the sender: Forsythe. His heart hammered like the recoil of an RPG. Beckett's last name.

His lungs required more air, but the pumping of his diaphragm couldn't keep up. Cole's hands felt the shape of whatever the envelope contained. Like a book. It brought him back to that last day when he saw Beckett stuff something in a package and shove it under his gear as if it were contraband.

"You got a girl back home, Forsythe?" Most of the guys had packages prepared to send to loved ones if anything happened to them.

A blush ran up Beckett's face. "No, sir."

Cole nodded to the gear hiding the package. "Then I bet your mom will cherish whatever's in that envelope." Though the hope was, it would never need to be sent.

"Yes, sir. She'd consider it very important."

"I'm heading to chow. Wanna come along?" Cole didn't know why, but he sensed he needed to spend some time with this young man.

Beckett stood, glanced back at his gear. "Yes, sir."

They headed to the hall, picked entrées from the choices in the line and sat across from each other at a table. Cole had grown to respect the Lance Corporal, even if he seemed a little different sometimes. He'd matured immensely since he'd first arrived in Iraq, and though Cole had worked him hard all those months ago, he knew he could not take credit for the man Beckett had become. He suspected it was something else that filled him and grew him. Maybe something his parents taught. Maybe something in that black, leather book he carried. Or maybe something gained in those moments on his knees. Cole almost envied him.

Beckett closed his eyes as Cole had seen him do many times before a meal. The guys said he had to bless it before he ate. But this blessing seemed to take an inordinate amount of time. Finally, Beckett's lids lifted and he grabbed a fork.

Cole was halfway through his burger already. "Hope you put in a good word with the Big Guy for me."

Beckett stared into his plate as he sawed his chicken. "Always, sir."

Cole flinched. He was only kidding. Did Beckett really pray for him regularly? "Guess that means I'll survive another day in combat." He picked up a chip.

"No, sir."

Cole dropped the chip.

"I ... I mean, that's not all I pray for. I don't only pray we stay safe." He hesitated, then swallowed hard, as he kept his eyes low. "Some of us will die. We've seen that." He shrugged. "This is war after all." Beckett stirred at the rice with his fork. "It just makes sense to pray for more than mere survival."

Cole choked on his soda. "More than mere survival? Without survival nothing else matters."

Beckett's green eyes reached deep when they captured Cole's gaze. "Sir," Beckett's voice held authority and humility at the same time, "don't you believe there's something more?"

"What? You mean like heaven?"

"Yes."

Cole wasn't sure he liked the turn of this conversation. "I guess I wonder sometimes."

"There is, sir." He stopped, looked around and opened his mouth, but Cole stood and collected his tray.

"I know where the chaplain is, Lance Corporal." Cole didn't need to be preached to by some pimple-faced enlisted man.

Beckett's gaze dropped to his plate. "Sorry, sir. I thought you wanted to know."

Cole turned back. Beckett was a good Marine. He didn't deserve to be dismissed. Cole dropped his tray on the table and sat back down. He'd let him air his beliefs tonight—if he must. "What is it you want to tell me?"

Beckett sucked from his soda straw. "It's just that ... you never seem happy, sir."

Cole laughed out loud. "You mean here," he gestured around, "in the middle of a war zone with a bunch of men who hate me because I want to increase their chances of staying alive?"

"Yeah, sir. I mean, other guys laugh and joke about stuff. Even the officers." Beckett seemed to be talking to his rice. He glanced up. "But you always look like you're ready to eat fire."

Cole glared.

Beckett flinched, and dropped his gaze. "Like now."

Cole drew in a breath and tried to relax his jaw muscles. "What are you getting at, Forsythe?"

"Why are you here, sir?"

Cole surveyed the look on his Lance Corporal's face. "You've become awfully bold this evening, son."

Beckett's expression took on a melancholy that froze Cole. Like he knew something terrible that he couldn't share. And Cole didn't want to know what it was.

"Sometimes a person needs to speak when they have the time. War makes you realize how short that time can be."

"And you feel you need to speak to me?"

Beckett's shoulders, which had broadened since they'd first met, rose and fell on a slow wave. "Why are you here, sir?"

"To kill the enemy. Same as you." Something about the kid tonight glued Cole to the seat. Why did he feel he needed to hear what Beckett had to say?

"Sergeant over there says you're stinkin' rich."

"Yeah, so?"

"I just don't get why a rich guy would join the Marines."

Cole speared him with his eyes. He didn't need to lay out his misfortune to this man-boy. "What? Rich guys can't be patriotic? They attacked our country."

Beckett lifted a shoulder. "I don't know. It just seems like you're looking for something, but never finding it."

"Like what?" Cole hadn't been probed like this since Joe Sakamoto.

"Order. Purpose. Maybe acceptance."

Cole raised a brow. "Acceptance? You think I joined the Marines for acceptance?"

"Yeah. You know—'got each other's back,' 'leave no man behind'—that sort of thing. Like family."

Cole considered his parents for the briefest of seconds. "I don't need family."

"Everyone needs family."

"Well, I have none."

Beckett's grin grew in its inanity. "You've got me."

So much for Beckett as family. In less than twenty-four hours, that relationship had been blown to bits—literally.

Cole's intact hand now ran the length of the package obviously mailed by Beckett's family. What could they have sent him? The lettering on the outside did not resemble Beckett's chicken scratch. Cole would know that mess anywhere. This couldn't be the same package Beckett had sealed that last night. But now, Cole wondered about that one too. It seemed Beckett had been without his black, leather book at his cot afterward. Very strange for him. Had God punished him for his neglect?

If there was a God.

Cole should open the package and discover its contents, but his myo-electric arm buzzed as he gripped it hard, reminding him of what made that action difficult. What made the idea impossible. His intact fingers ran over the name, Forsythe, and over the ridge of the seal. His jaw flexed and he tossed the package deep into his closet.

His mind traveled to Beckett's expression when he'd caught Cole later that night downing a bottle of whiskey he'd bought from an Iraqi boy. It wasn't censure. It wasn't even disappointment. Somehow, it was almost a confirmation of what was to come.

Like he knew.

Cole shuddered. He would never open that package. He didn't need a reminder of his failings. His own body displayed those failings every day. His mind whirred in a painful montage of past and present. What would he do with the envelope at the bottom of his closet? He wasn't sure. The only thing for certain was that he couldn't face its contents sober.

~*~

Why had Carly put on eyeliner and blush? Why was she wearing this pale yellow sundress that clung to her form? And why was she brushing her hair as if it might shine at the hundredth stroke?

She kept telling herself it was only proper to dress for dinner given Cole had worn his best each night since they'd begun eating together two months ago. But she knew it was more. She felt something real and tangible in the man who slew her dragon. The knight who wore his armor against those who'd love him, leaving himself vulnerable to the things that might mean his end. If only she could reverse that. But she knew she did not have the power and even if she did, it would only leave him indebted to her and not the God he so desperately needed. The God who would be there for him when she could not.

The God who'd brought Cole into her father's life. And hers.

She stepped into the dining room, wobbling on the low heels. Cole sat filling his mouth using a fork while reading a book. He looked up and choked, dribbles of food spilling over his lips.

She scanned the front of her outfit. "Is something wrong?"

He cleared his throat and wiped his mouth with a linen napkin. "You're wearing a dress."

Why did he look like he'd seen an aberration? Carly wanted to flee.

He waved her in. "Don't just stand there. Mrs. Rivera's keeping your dinner warm." His features softened with a crooked smile, his eyes warming as he observed every inch of her. "I guess now we know what took you so long."

Heat rose in her cheeks. She sat at the table and shook out the linen napkin.

Mrs. Rivera came through the swinging door carrying her dinner plate. "Oh, Carly, you look lovely tonight. Is that a new dress?"

"No. The only dresses I own are sundresses. The weather's warming."

"You should wear them more often." She shot a look toward Cole. "Don't you think, Mr. Cole?"

His gaze had not wavered from her. "Yes."

Carly looked into her plate as Mrs. Rivera exited. The heat of Cole's eyes singed and chilled her at the same time. She shivered.

"Should I turn down the air conditioning, Beauty?" The moniker held a tenderness she'd never heard before.

She studied her meal—pork chops, twice-baked potato and broccoli.

He lifted his myo-electric arm. It buzzed into a pointing position. "I can practice pushing the thermostat buttons. It'd be no problem. Like therapy."

Carly spied the grin on his face and mirrored it back to him. He'd become so accustomed to his new limbs and seemed to really appreciate the difference they made in his life, drawing her into his accomplishments.

"I'm fine. Really."

He forked a broccoli spear and chewed, still watching her.

She needed to talk to him about her father, not sure how Cole would take her request. After tasting each part of her meal, she put her fork in her plate, her hands in her lap and plunged ahead. "I don't know if you've been watching the news, lately."

"Yes."

"The trial against my father's company starts in a couple weeks."

"Yes, I saw that."

"There are murmurs he might be brought up on criminal neglect charges in the case of the Marine who died."

"That's just bluster." Cole shook his head. "Lawyers threaten to drag as many names through the mud as they can to make the public see how wronged the victim is."

Carly's nose tingled. It wasn't just bluster to her and she knew it wasn't bluster to her father, either. His reputation was on the line.

"They'll give up on pursuing criminal charges, making the monetary raping by the plaintiff look as though it were forgiving."

How could he be so cold to a family who lost their dad? "My father feels for these people." Which is what made the situation more tenuous for him.

Cole tilted his head.

She swallowed the lump in her throat. "But he does not deserve to be held criminally responsible for something he had no part of."

Cole took a sip from his milk. "I sense you're telling me this for a reason."

She reached for the cross at her neck. "I need to be with my father through the trial."

~*~

It hit Cole like an RPG, exploding the carefully constructed shelter he'd built around himself. "You're leaving?"

"Not leaving. Just taking some time off. I've—"

"Is this because of what happened this afternoon? On the hike?" How could he have been so stupid?

Carly's fingers rubbed at the cross like a charm. "No. No. I just need to be with my father right now."

Would she tell her father about Cole's suggestion of a kiss? Would she ask his advice on whether or not to allow a relationship with him? What was he thinking? Carly was looking for a reason to escape, and not a temporary one. She wanted to jump the train and never look back. Here, he'd hoped she'd dressed up for him—stupid.

Could he keep her at the manor? "What about rehab? We were going to work on the fine motor skills for the hand."

"I've already spoken to Sam."

"Yes, I saw you having lunch with him on the patio yesterday." Why did his voice sound so bitter, so jealous? He had to keep up his guard.

"We were discussing him taking over your rehab in addition to the hippotherapy."

"Without consulting me first?"

"I wanted to put the pieces together before I considered going."

"I see." Cole worked the muscles in his face not to show disappointment.

Her gaze rummaged it like she planned to memorize every turn of his expression. "I don't think you do."

"You need a real break. More than an escape into a book."

Carly's eyes remained locked with his. "Why do you assume people want to leave you? Do you have any idea how much you are loved?"

Was she saying she—?

"Your staff would crawl over broken glass for you."

His staff. That statement hurt more than the severing of limbs. "They're paid well to do so."

Her chuckle fled a twisted grin. "They're not paid *that* well."

Cole didn't know whether to seethe or sneer. He did both.

"They're here because they love you. I've never seen a family love their children as much as your staff loves you. There's a fondness between you and them that is so warm I can feel the heat whenever I'm in the room. I see it in their eyes when they speak of you."

"And what do their eyes say?" Pity.

"They speak of the boy within the man. The generosity buried beneath bitterness and self-absorption."

"Self-absorption?" How dare they?

"Actually, I added that part myself." Such cockiness in those brown eyes tonight. He could no longer allow himself to be captured by them.

"Cole, you have so much empty junk in your life you can't see over it to the happiness others have with so much less."

Cole threw his napkin on the table and hoisted himself out of the chair.

"That's right. Leave when you don't like the truth."

He turned. "If I'm so awful, then why do all these people supposedly love me so much?"

"I never said you were awful."

Cole plopped back into the upholstered dining chair.

"In fact, it's those little teeny," she emphasized the last word through bare teeth, "glimpses of the man underneath, that draws us all to hope for more."

Why did his pulse race at the word "us?" "You're saying they hope one day I'll be nice to them?"

"No, Cole." Her eyes melted into him. "Their hope is for you to be nice to yourself."

"What do you want me to do?"

"Accept the love they give you. And allow yourself to love them in return."

What did that even mean? Cole had no clue.

"And accept God's love."

"So He can punish me for hating Him?" Where did that come from? He didn't even believe in God.

Pain seemed to course through Carly's expression before her lids lowered and rose. Her eyes searched his in a way that made him feel raw. Her lips parted on a breath. "While we were still sinners, Christ died for us." She whispered the words as if she'd said this phrase a thousand times. As if it was engraved on her soul.

Died for us. He'd seen that type of sacrifice up close. It was the thorn he could never remove. The life he did not deserve. And yet Carly placed herself as the recipient of the same kind of sacrifice. What did she know about being responsible for someone else's death?

Died for us.

A tear slid down her face. "Are you going to allow me to be with my father?"

He'd let his anger get out of control again. Would he always regret his words? "You are not a prisoner here. You can come and go as you please."

"But our agreement? Will you still honor—?"

"Of course."

She flinched at his sharp tone.

Carly was right. He was self-absorbed. "Your father needs you. Go to him." Cole lifted himself from the seat. "As long as necessary. Sam is a good occupational therapist. He'll take care of me. In fact, if you feel you can't come back—don't bother." He strode out the door.

Chapter Twelve

"Why are you saddling my father's horse?" Cole's tone came out more accusatory than he'd meant it to.

Joe Sakamoto turned. "You know I like to work them out daily."

"You're going to ride him?"

Joe adjusted the stirrups on the chestnut gelding. "No, Sam is."

Cole noticed the empty stall. "And where's Miss Gray?"

"Carly's riding her."

"What?" That, he couldn't believe.

Joe swatted the dust from his hands. "Sam's taking Carly around the field on Miss Gray to prepare her for a ride through the woods." Joe's eyes didn't leave Cole's, as if he was gauging Cole's reaction.

"How'd he get her on a horse?" Cole couldn't imagine the woman extracting her arms from around her body long enough to climb in the saddle, let alone not yelp when it moved.

"You'll have to ask Sam that question." Amusement sparked Joe's eyes. "He can be very persuasive when he wants to be."

Yeah. Cole bet he could, and that made him all the more uneasy. He headed out to the field where Sam was leading Miss Gray and Carly toward the stable. Sam talked incessantly as Carly chuckled between bouts of stiffness when the animal stepped into a small hole, unsettling her in the saddle. She occasionally even giggled at herself.

The look of intensity whenever Carly clutched the horn tighter would have entertained Cole had it not been interrupted by the jovial banter of the occupational therapist.

She smiled at something Sam said, then looked up to see Cole.

The smile vanished.

Cole strode toward them, his prosthetic toe catching the edge of a hole, locking his knee. Sam stepped as if to catch him, but Cole recovered. "I hear you two are riding today."

Sam patted the horse, his ever-present grin larger than usual. It grated on Cole's nerves. "Carly agreed to ride if I took over your rehab while she's gone."

Cole looked between the two. Carly stared at her whitened knuckles around the horn.

"That's a big price to pay, Beauty, so you can get outta Dodge."

Sam's face sobered. "Or so your therapy won't be interrupted."

Cole smirked. "You get more like your father every day, Sam."

"Thank you."

"If you don't want us to ride ..." Carly turned to slide from the horse.

"Oh, no. Don't use me as an excuse to get off that horse. You made your agreement with the man. Now you should ride with him."

"She's not riding with me." Sam nodded toward the stable.

Lightning whinnied as Joe led her to join them.

"She's riding with you."

"But—" Was that panic in Carly's eyes? "You said you'd take me through the trails."

"I said you'd have an expert rider with you the whole time." By the look on the faces of father and son, it was clear they were cooking up trouble. "And you will."

~*~

Carly couldn't read Cole. Would he ride with her or walk away? He seemed to speak a curse to each Sakamoto with his eyes before he took Lightning's reins.

He stepped his right foot into the stirrup, held the horn in his left hand and swung the prosthesis over the horse. Carly marveled at the way he'd balanced the leg in the air so it would bend and straighten with the force of gravity to make the move so fluid. The muscles in his arm and shoulders flexed and relaxed under his gray t-shirt.

The tension in the air between them seemed to sizzle and zap as Joe and Sam sauntered toward the stable apparently sharing a joke.

"Let's go." Cole clucked and nudged his horse to move.

Carly clucked and nudged, but Miss Gray stood still.

Cole turned back. "What's wrong?"

"She won't budge."

"Didn't Sam teach you what to do?"

"Yeah, but she won't listen to me."

Cole led his horse back as if it were an extension of his natural limbs. "What did you do?"

"I did this." Carly shifted forward.

"Use your knees more. Give a little kick."

"I don't want to hurt her."

Cole sighed deep. "I didn't mean kick her hard. Just a thump. "He demonstrated on Lightning. "Like this." The horse stepped around her.

Carly imitated as best she could. Miss Gray jerked forward, startling her. "Whoa."

Miss Gray halted.

"I didn't mean stop-whoa."

Cole's face broke into a smile. He turned away, but Carly could still hear him snicker.

He faced her again, lips seeming to fight a twitch. "Nudge her again so we can be on our way. And don't say—uh—that word again."

Carly nudged and thumped and clucked, and even gave the reins a little shake. The horse moved and they were on their way.

Cole turned Lightning to the trail, his body moving in an easy lope with the horse. "Don't forget to lean with the hills and guide the horse away from the trees. Otherwise you'll hit your knees."

Carly pulled the reins just in time for her leg to miss a trunk. She released a breath.

"Remember, Miss Gray will go where you lead her. If that's scraping a tree with your leg, that's what she'll do."

"Great." She maneuvered past another close one. "Could you find a wider path, then?"

"This is the one that takes us where I want to go."

And where would that be? She scanned the innards of the forest, growing denser. The lair of a beast?

Cole led them up an incline. Carly leaned forward as Miss Gray took the hill, her heart pounding at the way the horse jerked with the climb. Why was she doing this?

The forest was close with early summer growth. The breeze hissed through the leaves, fluttering like millions of tiny serpent's tongues, branches reaching out as if to steal her from the horse. She almost wished they would, and save her from this ride.

A faint trickle of water sounded from far away. It calmed her.

Cole turned into another path then down a slight hill. Carly leaned back trying not to slide forward in the saddle and pulled the reins for Miss Gray to follow him. Could she trust this animal to get her to their destination unscathed?

They turned again. The sound of water stronger as they mounted a small hill and came over the rise. There it was. A crystal clear stream cutting a meandering path through the forest floor, tripping over rocks and carrying fallen foliage downstream. A frog croaked, a squirrel scurried and a bird sang.

Cole swung off his horse and led it to the water. He walked around Miss Gray and held her still as Carly dismounted, glad to be on solid ground again. Cole's lip twitched at the deep sigh she'd released before she'd thought to hide it.

He sat at the edge of the brook. Carly scrambled beside him. He picked up a stone and threw it in. It splashed. Would he speak to her after all she'd said to him the night before?

"I'm sorry about how I reacted at dinner." Cole threw another stone into the stream. A frog jumped from the mud.

"I'm sorry about what I said. I had no right." Carly tossed a stone in herself.

The music of the water filled the silence. Carly let it run over her, giving her a moment of peace and contentment. But there was something unfinished between them.

"You never told me what happened to Beckett." She wanted Cole to know she was still there for him. She still cared.

He remained silent.

Carly turned to watch him stare into the water as if it would speak answers for him.

"I don't know if I can." The words were barely audible.

"Try."

~*~

Cole's gaze met Carly's for a good long while before he rested it back on the stream. "You might as well know."

Her words last night had convicted him. She spoke truth about his self-absorption, but there was no goodness underneath.

"I'm not the generous dragon-slayer you think my staff believes me to be." Each breath unlocked a treasure of pain, unearthed by his words. "Beckett died because of my recklessness."

"Cole, men die in war. It comes with the territory."

She didn't understand.

"No." His face burned with internal rage. "He didn't die because we were outmaneuvered or undermanned." His jaw grew ridged, his breath in long, drawn-out heaves.

The concern on Carly's face pulled him in, made him want to tell her. He'd lose her for sure when she found out, but maybe that was for the best.

"We were directed to a house by an informant. Insurgents were suspected to have gathered there." He swallowed the bile rising from his gut. "I checked the perimeter before we entered, in case it was a set up—a booby trap." Cole's head ached as if he were still hung over from that day. "I could barely complete a clear thought that morning. I'd been drinking the night before and was still feeling its effects."

Carly stared. Confusion, pity or censure, he couldn't tell.

"I lumbered around, not scanning the terrain as I normally would. This informant was a good one, so I counted on his information being solid, that no one was there. Not a smart strategy in war, and not one I would have followed sober." He licked his parched lips. "In the hospital, when I woke, minus two limbs, I'd been told Beckett had seen a man with a cell phone on the roof across the street, and before he could yell for me to run, he threw himself on the backpack IED, effectively absorbing the blow saving all the Marines around him."

Carly's little gasp jolted Cole. He stared at his shoes. "I was the only one left with injuries. Becket, on the other hand, was left with nothing." The confounded tear escaped. He squeezed his facial muscles trying to stop the burning in his eyes and nose. He buried his face in his arms, resting on his bent legs. "He sacrificed his life for mine, because I was too drunk to be vigilant."

The sound of the water rushed his eardrums. Cole wished it could wash him away. Or at least wash away the stain of his guilt. But Cole knew nothing could bring Becket back from the grave.

The gentle touch on his shoulder startled him. The scent of coconut nearing. Carly didn't speak. He didn't want her to, but her presence gave him a sort of calm.

She hadn't left.

He lifted from his position. "We better get back."

Carly stood close and held his arm to still him. She placed her hand on his cheek. He held it there with his own. She pulled up on her tip toes. Was she going to … ?

Her lips brushed his. He moved his mouth with hers, taking in the scent of coconut and fresh pine. She pressed closer into him and kissed the scar at his lip and the line up his cheek. Cole placed his hand on her face and led her lips back to his. They worked together as if they'd known each other a very long time.

Carly pulled back and took in a deep breath.

His fingers went to the disfigurement of his face, remembering the feel of her lips against it. "It's still there." He couldn't help but grin, thinking of their fairytale. "The Beauty's kiss was supposed to change me."

She shook her head, and whispered, "I can't change you."

He tapped his myo-electric arm. "But you've made me whole."

Carly winced. "No, Cole. Only God can make you whole."

He jolted and pivoted on his good leg. She had to ruin the moment with that word. "I don't want your God."

Chapter Thirteen

Cole bolted up from his bed sucking in air as if it were his last. His chest filled and emptied.

Up—Down.

Up—Down.

He scanned the room. The shelves of classic novels his grandfather had amassed over his lifetime had stood sentry since before it had been his father's study.

He was safe. Not in Iraq. No IEDs or rapid machine-gun fire. Still, the image of Beckett's body dispersing in a cloud of smoke haunted his waking vision. He hadn't even seen the explosion in real life, but it replayed in his mind's eye just the same.

Would it ever be erased?

His diaphragm labored against the breath that struggled to fill his lungs. He scrubbed his face with his intact hand. The package seemed to call from his closet.

No. Cole wouldn't go there. But until he destroyed it, he would never rest. He flung off his sheets and scrambled to the floor, crawling—two limbs, two stumps—until he made it to the closet. He dug past the shoes and boxes on the floor then found the package and scanned the name again.

Forsythe.

Closing his eyes against the lettering, he dropped his head. He couldn't destroy it. It'd be like murdering Beckett all over again. Cole would have to open it.

Eventually.

~*~

"Manny, I need you to drive me somewhere." Cole stood at the open door of the chauffer's garage apartment.

Manny blinked, ran his hand through his bed-head, and yawned big. He peered at his watch. "It's six in the morning."

Cole shifted his weight to the prosthetic leg. "I know what time it is. I need to get to the liq—"

Manny's eyes shot wide.

"I mean, you need to take me into Fairwilde."

Manny shook his head. "Man!" he spat. "I thought you were gonna do it this time. I thought you were gonna stay sober."

Cole fumed. "You don't know anything. I need to get into town."

Manny's gaze held firm. "I know that look. Same one my father had when he 'needed' a bar." He checked his watch again. "The liquor store isn't even open yet, but you think you need to go now."

Cole ground his teeth and almost hissed. He scanned through the doorway at the text books stacked beside Manny's computer. "What would happen if you lost your job and housing before you finished your on-line degree?"

Manny's mouth dropped open, but he stood taller as if to defend his position.

"I expect you dressed and ready to drive me by eight o'clock." Cole hobbled down the wooden stair case. "Otherwise your own car better be packed with your belongings."

~*~

Eight o'clock. Cole, now showered and ready for the day, came out to find Manny's VW Bug loaded, and Manny carrying a large, green trash bag. He glanced at Cole. "I'll have to come back for the rest of my stuff. It won't fit in my car."

Cole's nostrils flared. This was not what he had in mind. "What are you doing?"

"I'm fired, right?" Manny shrugged. "I'm leavin'."

"Where're you going to live?"

Manny shrugged again. "I don't know. I'm hopin' maybe Sam'll take me in. He's pretty cool."

Yes. Everyone seemed to think Sam cool.

Cole narrowed his eyes. "You'd leave before taking me to a liquor store?"

Manny dropped the trash bag into his trunk. "Either that or become complicit in your alcoholism. After seeing you go through the DTs, man," he shook his head warily, "I'm not doin' that again."

Why had Cole allowed himself to be so exposed? "Become *complicit*?" His jaw ached as it oozed of sarcasm. "Such big words they teach on-line college students these days."

Manny stared at his feet.

"You're willing to lose your job rather than take me?"

Manny nodded, still watching the ground.

"You have nowhere to go. Fairwilde isn't teeming with opportunities."

"I'm not taking you."

"Then give me the keys to the limo."

"Joe's got 'em."

"What?" Cole seethed. Manny knew Cole would never get them from Joe. He stomped back toward the manor, but stopped at the edge of the drive and turned. "Go back to your garage, Manny. You need me too much." Cole waited until Manny raised his eyes.

Your staff would crawl over broken glass for you, Cole.

Cole straightened to full height. "Just know this, I don't need you." He pivoted and entered the side door. He strode through the hall to his bedroom, lifted the cordless phone off the receiver, and punched in Jurvis's number.

"Hello."

"Jurvis, I have a job for you."

"What's that?"

Cole listed off the items he'd been craving over the past month.

Jurvis sighed contentment. "It's about time. I'll be there as soon as possible."

~*~

Cole had waited by the side entrance, but would not allow Jurvis to come in. He'd send Jurvis on his way after he retrieved the bags of goodies he'd ordered.

"The others don't know yet, huh?"

Cole grasped the sack and shook his head. Why did it feel so underhanded to do what one wanted to do?

"If you'd like, I could take you out to lunch. Have some drinks there."

Cole shook his head again. "Got business here to tend to."

"Maybe another time, then."

"Sure." Cole stomped through the door and toward his room before anyone could discover what he carried. He hid one bag under his bed and opened the other.

Scotch. His old friend.

He drew in a breath and cracked the seal of the bottle, licking his lips like a starving lion.

It burned as it first slid down his throat, but seemed to fill gaps aching for its sustenance. He sighed deep and hard, before taking another swallow.

The closet door didn't seem so ominous now. One more sip, and he could open it, rummage for the package, and uncover its horrors.

He tilted the bottle and swallowed ... and swallowed ... and swallowed, again ... until the bottle was drained.

Cole dropped it to the floor, licked the remainder of liquor from his lips and closed his eyes relishing the last drops on his tongue.

He walked across the floor, toward the closet, but his prosthesis seemed to protest against the working of his mind. Had he forgotten how to make the leg move?

He'd get there if he had to crawl.

The door squeaked as he hinged it opened. He dropped to his good knee and lifted the envelope from the floor.

The name taunted him so he held fast with the myo-electric grip and shredded the paper with his left hand like an animal devouring its prey.

There was nothing left of the envelope. Only the black, leather book it contained, and a piece of paper sticking out from the pages, folded over the title: *The Holy Bible*.

Cole swallowed as he struggled to control the burn in his eyes, his nose, his throat. He opened the cover and read the name written in a familiar chicken scratch: Beckett Forsythe. Why had someone sent him this book?

Cole pulled the paper from inside. He'd gone this far, he might as well open that too.

"What are you doing to me, Beckett?" He pressed the letter flat. "Will you ever let me be?"

The handwriting was tidy. Not Beckett's. Who could have sent this? He scanned the missive to find out.

Dear Second Lt. Harrison,

I'm sure you are wondering why we are sending our son, Beckett Forsythe's, Bible to you at this time. You see, it was his request we do so upon his death. I'm sorry to say when we first received it so many years ago with instructions on his wishes, I could not part with it. Beckett, being my only child, it was all I had left of the man who'd gone off to war and it was a reminder he'd remained strong in his faith till the end. Notions like that give a mother much comfort, because it reminds me I will see him again one day.

Please forgive me my selfishness, taking so long to honor his wishes. I needed time to read through the passages he'd underlined since becoming a Marine and run my finger over his notes in the margins. I'd missed the boy he'd grown from, but now had an opportunity to meet the man he'd become.

I understand why he'd want you to have his most prized possession. He'd often spoken of you and how you'd helped him become a better Marine. As his mother, I am truly grateful. I suspect you may have had something to do with the maturity of his faith since he left home. Otherwise he wouldn't have wanted you to have this gift.

Again, please forgive me for holding it from you for so long. Beckett's father and I would love to meet you some day. If you are ever in town, you are welcome as our honored guest.

Sincerely,
Julia Forsythe

Cole leaned back against the side of the bed and heaved reluctant oxygen into his lungs.

Honored guest? She'd spit in his face if she knew the truth.

The maturity of his faith? Ha!

Cole crunched the letter in his fist and peered heavenward. "I hate You." How could he hate something that didn't exist? Or did it? "Why are you taunting me, God?"

He lifted the black book to fling it across the room, but a section of pages dropped out from the middle. He picked up the unbound section of the book and peered at the title across the first of its pages.

Psalms. Beckett's favorite. Written by the warrior king. Was his name David?

Cole tossed the pages and the book on his bed and exited the room.

~*~

Carly came from the kitchen and almost ran into him. "Cole. Where're you going?"

He continued on, heading out the back patio door, the lingering scent of alcohol in his wake. She followed.

He strode with force and purpose toward the stable.

"Cole!"

He didn't turn. Something was very wrong. Carly was set to leave the next day, and she suspected Cole had had a relapse.

He entered the stable. Carly heard his and Joe's voices in heated debate. She opened the door.

"You'll ride Lightning drunk over my dead body." Joe stood a good six inches shorter than the ex-Marine who'd made a point to tower over him. With or without limbs, there was no doubt Cole could fulfill Joe's wishes.

Cole balled his fist and seemed to consider the option. He skirted left. Joe blocked him. He skirted right to find Joe there again.

"Out of my way."

Joe didn't budge.

"This is my property."

"Do you hear yourself, Cole? You sound like a spoiled little boy."

"And you're not my father."

The words seemed to stab Joe. "Then fire me."

Cole's jaw hardened. "Don't tempt me."

Joe stood taller.

"You can't stand here all day."

Joe glowered.

"Fine." Cole pivoted and strode past Carly as though she weren't even there. "I'll be back," he called over his shoulder.

Chapter Fourteen

Carly packed her car to the gills with every last bit of her things. Tempted to leave behind a book or two—a statement she'd be back—she changed her mind, reasoning she might need something to read at the courthouse between hearings. It was as if something here drew her and frightened her at the same time? The sound of the trunk slamming shut thumped through her bones—like the period at the end of a sentence.

"Got everything?" Joe approached from the long drive.

"Yep. I guess it's time to go." A hollowness echoed through her. Was it really time to go? She thought of Cole's drunken behavior yesterday. There seemed to be so much unfinished business. Did he regret their kiss? Did she?

"How long will you be away?"

She blew a strand of hair from her face. "No telling how long the trial will take." Her gaze seemed to drift past Joe on its own hoping to see some movement inside, telling her someone else would come out to say goodbye.

"He's asleep." Joe answered the question she wouldn't ask. "Or passed out. Not really sure. He had one drained bottle on his nightstand, another untouched."

Why did she want to sob on Joe's shoulder right now? "Is he drinking because I'm leaving?"

"No. You didn't cause this. Mrs. Rivera says he's been acting strange since he got a package the other day."

Carly shifted. "A package? What was in it?"

"No one knows."

She shook her head. "It feels wrong leaving now. Maybe I can do something. Help him. Challenge him again."

Joe placed a hand on her shoulder. "No. You've done all you can. You need to be with your father, now."

"But—"

Joe raised a palm. "You can't let his drinking rule your decisions."

"I don't want to leave him like this."

Joe's smile was melancholy. He searched her face as if knowing all that was in her heart. How she felt about the man she would not see for a very long time. "Leave this one to God, Carly. I believe He's called you away because He needs to do this work with Cole alone."

"But Cole doesn't believe in God."

Joe chuckled. "That's what he keeps saying. It's his way of telling God, 'talk to the hand' when in reality he's just mad. He needs to get over his tantrum and finally hash it out with his Creator."

Carly's shoulders fell. "He won't do that."

"Oh, yeah? Then why did I find him in bed asleep with a Bible on his nightstand and loose pages of it beside him?"

"Loose pages?"

"Yeah, like they'd fallen out from over use."

Could she hope? "Where'd he get a Bible?"

"Who knows." Joe opened her car door. "Don't worry about Cole. You take care of your dad."

She sighed long and hard as she stepped into the vehicle.

"And don't forget to pray."

~*~

Cole pried his eyes open one at a time. Boy, was that sunlight bright. He should have pulled the blinds before he'd fallen asleep reading the tiny type and worn notes of Beckett's psalms. He hadn't even thought of sleep. It just took him on its own.

His tongue stuck to the roof of his mouth as he peered at the clock's LED display—12:07PM. Half the day gone already.

Was Carly gone too? He groaned at the thought of missing someone who never really belonged to him. His fingers touched the side of his face, remembering the tenderness of her lips against his scar—like maybe she could love every part of him. Or maybe she had only pitied him.

Why let people in when they only left?

The amber liquid of the Jim Beam bottle behind the clock came into focus. He unstuck his tongue and wet his lips. A shot glass sat beside the bottle—unused. He'd brought it from the kitchen hoping to feel less savage in his attempts to slay another bottle from the stash Jurvis had bought him, but the bottle had yet to be opened. The black, leather book sat in front of it.

Beckett's pages. Where were they? He lifted the comforter, the sheets. Nothing. The pillow beside him. A deep sigh escaped as he grasped them from the mattress.

It was only then Cole noticed the dull ache in his head. A bottle of scotch will do that to you. He placed the palm of his intact hand over the front of the Psalms, then ran his fingers over the notes in the margins—the ones Beckett's mother had cherished. The ones that taught her about the man he'd become. Cole had spent the last part of the day and into the night reading through those pages and deciphering the handwriting, trying to make sense of the young man who sought death to save him.

Why would anyone do that? Beckett had everything to live for—a family who loved him. And yet he risked it all to extend a useless life.

Even though I walk through the valley of the shadow and death ...

Why did those words keep playing in Cole's mind?

... I will fear no evil ...

He couldn't make them stop.

... for you are with me ...

Please, make them stop.

... your rod and your staff, they comfort me.

Cole looked to the bottle again and considered its contents. He ground his teeth and closed his eyes.

"Not now," he hissed as he flung off his sheets, grabbed the crutch by the bed, and hobbled to the shower.

~*~

"You're awake, Mr. Cole." Was that shock or accusation in Joe's eyes?

Cole strode to Lightning's stall, a backpack slung over his shoulder. "No, I'm not drunk." He might as well get that question out of the way.

"Um. Okay."

"And I will take my horse out today." He glared at the man. "If you don't mind."

Joe held his hands in surrender. "Fine with me." He backed away and entered another stall. "Carly left this morning."

Cole jolted. He'd already checked the suite that seemed vacuous without her things. Then why did Joe's words sting? The sound of Joe mucking out the stall told him Joe didn't expect a reply. Good, he didn't plan to give one.

The Bible practically sizzled in Cole's grip as he transferred it from the backpack to the saddlebag hanging from the horse. No sense letting Joe see it. That would prompt too many questions Cole had no answers for.

He mounted Lightning and rode along the path he'd taken the other day with Carly, the words from that book playing in his head like a song:

He makes me lie down in green pastures, He leads me beside quiet waters, He restores my soul.

Why did Cole absorb these words as though his soul were parched? How many times had he heard them before? The Twenty-third Psalm. Too many to count. How many times had he dismissed them, rolled his eyes at words meant to preach at him? Yet today they spoke something he needed to hear. Wanted to hear.

Ached to hear.

And all those other psalms. Some praising God—the God Cole wanted to despise. But others cried out to Him in distress. And still others even wondered where God was in times of trouble.

Yes, God. Where were you the day Beckett fell on an IED to save me?

I was there.

Cole sucked in a breath and looked around. No one. His eyes and nose burned, knowing the voice came from within. It couldn't be drowned out if he wanted to. His heart slammed against his chest.

I was there.

"Then why didn't you do something?"

A bird flew from a branch as though startled by Cole's booming question.

He slipped off his horse by the stream and sat where he had the day he told Carly about Beckett's death. Opening the pages of the black, leather book, he searched for references to the warrior king who wrote the psalms—David. He had no idea where to begin so he started in the section most heavily marked in Beckett's hand—1 Samuel. He flipped back to the beginning of the book and read.

He read of Samuel—the prophet. Of Saul—the king. And finally came to the shepherd boy.

The Lord is my shepherd. I shall not want.

Cole read by the stream, the water trickling past, until the light began to dim behind the thick, forest growth. Lightning whinnied, telling Cole it was time to get back.

He rode the trail thinking of the shepherd-turned-warrior-king and how like Beckett he was. A man after God's own heart. No wonder Beckett had identified with him. Though he strayed, he always came back to the Lord.

Unlike Cole, who'd never really known God in the first place.

Chapter Fifteen

"Hey, Mr. Cole. Join us for some hoops."

Just what Cole needed right now. A friend-fest where Manny fawned all over Sam.

"Yeah, Mr. Cole. Let's see what you got." Sam's eyes challenged just like his father's—the imp.

Manny tossed him the ball and Cole caught it. "On one condition."

Both pairs of eyes prompted him to tell.

"You stop calling me *Mr.* Cole."

Manny shrugged. "What are we supposed to call you then?" He looked oblivious.

Cole sighed. "I don't know. Your royal highness, maybe."

Manny's chin dropped.

"I'm just kidding, Manny. Call me Cole, please." He rolled the ball on his chest to his palm, then lobbed it toward the basket in a high arc—nothin' but net.

Manny whistled.

Sam caught it off a bounce. "Nice job—Cole." He glanced at Manny. "Hey, Manny and I are going to a concert tonight—NEEDTOBREATHE. A friend of mine had to bow out, so we have an extra ticket. Wanna come?"

Manny's brows rose as he shot Sam a questioning look.

Was Sam just being nice? Thinking Cole wouldn't accept? He'd call Sam's nice-guy bluff. "Sure, I'd love to." He stared, waiting for him to flinch.

Sam bounced the basketball. "Great. Be ready by six."

"Who's driving?"

Sam dribbled and shot. It bounced off the rim. "I am."

"I'd offer my limo, but I think my chauffeur's busy tonight."

Manny retrieved the ball beneath the hoop. "That's okay. I'll drive."

Sam looked between the two. He gestured to Cole. "You and me, being chauffeured by him?" He smirked at Manny. "Cool. Sounds like fun."

Cole turned toward the house. "See you boys at six."

~*~

Cole hadn't been to a rock concert in more than a decade. He watched the tree-lined mountain drive give way to Fairwilde's busy streets. Manny had the stereo pumping not just through the speakers, but the whole car seemed to buzz the bass line.

NEEDTOBREATHE. What kind of a name was that for a rock band? It didn't even have spaces between the words. What did the fan club call itself— THEASTHMATICS? Still, the music thudding through the limo felt good. Felt right. He might actually enjoy this concert.

Manny's gaze turned to the rearview. "How are you gentlemen doing back there?"

Sam rolled his eyes. "That's about the worst English accent I've ever heard." And it was.

"Hey, man. Can't blame a dude for tryin'." His gaze reflected in Cole's direction. "How 'bout you, Mr.—I mean—um, Cole."

"Doing fine."

Manny's eyes shifted as if he didn't believe him. "Want me to turn the music down?"

Now, he asks. "No." Cole didn't dare tap his fingers to the beat, feeling Sam and Manny watched his every move. He didn't want them to know he might be having a good time. He'd let them sweat a little longer.

"You're gonna love this concert, Cole. NEEDTOBREATHE is one of the best live bands going." Sam seemed to need to convince himself more than Cole.

"Right." Say just enough to keep them guessing.

Sam fidgeted in the leather seat. "You'd rather be on a horse right now, wouldn't you?"

"Nope. I'm good."

Sam sighed. "I remember, when I was a kid, watching you ride Lightning." He blew out a breath. Was he searching for conversation? "I was so jealous."

Jealous? "Why?"

"I would have loved to have ridden like that."

"Why didn't your father teach you?"

Sam's eyes turned to meet Cole's. "Well, he was kind of busy ... uh ... teaching you."

Cole's lids grew heavy. Please, not the poor-boy guilt stuff he always saw in the movies. "That was his job."

"No, Cole. It wasn't." Sam's tone hardened.

For some reason he almost wished Sam would use his title. More respect. "What do you mean?"

"He wasn't paid to teach you to ride. Your parents didn't even know he was doing it. He taught you after hours, because he wanted to."

Joe taught him in his spare time? Cole caught Manny's shocked look in the rearview before he focused back on the road. He seemed to try not to listen, but leaned back and turned his ear toward Cole just the same.

"Well, he eventually tired of it." A fresh stab of rejection hit Cole at the thought of how aloof Joe had become toward the end, just before Cole quit competing and began partying. What had Cole done to make Joe become so distant? He'd never figured it out, but it had haunted him for years.

Sam shrugged. "You and Lightning inspired me to ride." He chuckled. "But I had nowhere near your ability. So as they say, those who can't, teach. Or become hippotherapists."

He slumped in the seat and propped an ankle on his knee, seeming to relish the expansive leg room of the limo. "Still, watching you ride was magic. My friends and I all tried to imitate you. Even grew our hair longer like you used to wear it. But my mother said I looked like a girl, so she cut it." His smile tilted. "Couldn't pull off 'the manly' the way you did."

Cole bunched his brows. "That's funny, cause last I remember seeing you as a kid, you had a close cut, almost as bald as I am now. A new phase?"

Sam sobered and sat up. "No." He seemed to hesitate, his voice lowered. "That was after the chemo."

"Chemo?"

Manny's eyes shot wide in the rearview, mirroring Cole's thoughts.

"I fought cancer for a couple years. It was touch and go a few times."

"Cancer? How old were you?" Cole needed to know.

"Thirteen ..." He shrugged. "Maybe Fourteen."

Cole calculated. A weight fell over him. Was he that self-absorbed? Just like Carly said. He could barely speak. "That's why Joe stopped coaching me."

Sam almost looked guilty for taking his father back. "Yeah."

"But he never ..." Cole shook his head. "I asked him why he couldn't." His mind reeled with snatches of memories, conversations. "He said you were sick." Was that an elephant on his chest? "I thought you had a cold."

Sam's blink was slow. "It wasn't a cold."

"Why didn't he ... ?" Cole couldn't finish the question. He knew the answer. Joe hadn't told him because Cole never gave him the chance. He'd just raged on Joe as if he were a recalcitrant employee, not worthy of his pay, when in fact, he'd been worth so much more.

But why? Why did Joe do so much for him when he was a kid? And why did he stay with Cole even now?

You don't pay them that *much, Cole.*

Carly's words rang in his ears. He wished he could close them off, but they'd only be trapped inside to echo continuously against the walls of his skull.

Manny steered the limo into a parking garage and turned off the stereo. "Gentlemen. We have arrived at our destination." He tried cockney this time, tipping his invisible chauffeur's cap. "We, at Harrison's Limo Service, hope you enjoy your evening."

~*~

Cole waved to Manny as he ascended the stairs to his garage apartment.

Sam opened the door to his SUV. "You really had a good time, didn't you?"

"Yes, Sam, I really did." The first time he'd ever been to a concert, sans alcohol, and somehow he enjoyed it more.

Sam nodded. "I'm glad. Maybe we can do it again sometime. Third Day's coming next month."

Where did Sam hear of these bands? Cole wasn't that old and out of touch. "Sure. If they're half as good as your asthmatic group tonight, I might just like 'em."

Sam chuckled as he climbed into the vehicle. "Just make sure you bring robo-hand," he pointed to the myo-electric arm. "We'll have to teach you some new tricks for the fans."

Cole laughed. The image of the guy in the row behind them totally enamored at how Cole's wrist could do a 360, played in his mind. "Dude, do it again," he kept saying as he tapped another friend to watch. Finally, someone who appreciated the simple things.

Poor Jurvis.

The door clicked quietly open. No need to wake Mrs. Rivera. She'd need her sleep for another long day taking care of him and his over-large house. It was over-large, wasn't it? He really didn't need all that space, but downsizing would mean not needing the staff that cared for it, either. And he knew now, more than ever, he needed his staff.

Why did that scare him and bring him comfort at the same time? He couldn't be dependent on them. What if they left—like Carly? What if they died? Cole knew how tenuous life could be. Nothing was certain. If only there was one person he could count on to be there for him all the time.

I will be there for you, Cole.

Cole shook his head, his jaw firm. "I don't trust you, God." The words burned as they fell from his lips.

Cole didn't trust God. He was too unwieldy, uncontrollable. Why did others trust Him so much?

The Bible sat on the nightstand in his bedroom. The Jim Beam now in a bag under the bed. He considered the bottle, but the book called louder. Maybe he'd read about Jesus tonight. The New Testament. It couldn't hurt.

Chapter Sixteen

The bottles in the paper sack jangled as Cole carried them up the hill. He gritted his teeth, determined to follow through on his plan, knowing he'd receive the I-told-you-so look that always left him squirming like a petulant child.

Time to swallow some pride and admit defeat. He'd been wrong about Joe all these years. Joe hadn't abandoned him. He'd only needed to take care of his son. The son who'd almost died of cancer while Cole complained about not getting enough attention from the hired man.

The air in the stable felt close with dust and dirt from Joe's physical labor. Joe grunted as he pulled the saddle off Miss Gray and startled at the sight of Cole. "You okay?"

Cole shook his head and thrust the bags out. "Can you get rid of these?"

Joe's brow wrinkled as he accepted the sacks and peeked inside. "Why didn't you just pour them down the sink?"

Cole could hardly form the words. "Couldn't trust myself once they were opened."

"I'll take care of them."

Where was the lecture, the knowing look, or whatever Joe held in his arsenal of tutelage?

The crinkle surrounding Joe's almond-shaped eyes made Cole feel like a lost boy, needing to be found. "Is there more you need, Cole?"

Cole played with the myo-electric thumb, making it clack as he maneuvered it with the intact hand.

The man's stare reached deeper, as though it would find the thing Cole wanted to hide.

Releasing a breath, Cole plunged forward. "Can you give me the name of a counselor?"

Joe flinched.

"You know, someone who works with PTSD and substance abuse."

The stillness of the man made the wood paneling feel alive. "I don't know any."

Cole closed his eyes. He didn't want to just pick one from the phone book.

"Sam might have some contacts from his work at the clinic."

A sigh broke from Cole like the walls of an over-swelled levy.

"Is something wrong? Has my son been rude to you?"

"No. And that's just it. For a kid who seems to have despised me growing up, he's been nothing but kind."

"Despised you? Who told you that?"

"He did."

"When?"

"Last night." Cole peered down at the man. "He also told me about the cancer."

Joe grabbed a brush and ran it over Miss Gray's flank.

Cole shifted. "Why didn't you tell me?"

Joe's strokes were long and deliberate, seeming to take all his attention as they now traveled the length of the horse.

"Let me rephrase that." Cole gritted his teeth. "Why didn't you make me listen?"

Joe turned to catch Cole's gaze. The liquid shine in his eyes communicated more than words could.

The lump in Cole's throat was hard to push down. "I'm so sorry I treated you like that." He tried to swallow it again. "It was wrong of me. You never deserved the things I said to you."

Joe touched his eye as though something had fallen into it. His blink seemed to strain his features. The man turned back to the horse, his shoulders heaving with every breath, and strangled out, "Apology accepted."

~*~

"Carly, don't you worry about Mr. Cole." Mrs. Rivera's accent over the phone always made Carly smile. "He will not need Sam's therapy much longer, he is doing so well."

Something about her words left a hollow place in Carly's soul.

"He can hold a paper cup without collapsing it and made me scrambled eggs yesterday, cracking the shells with his metal hand."

Carly laughed at the idea of Cole serving her. She envisioned the pride in Mrs. Rivera's eyes as she accepted a dish of runny yellow goo made crunchy with fallen eggshells.

"He even went to a rock concert with Sam and Manny a few weeks ago."

Carly would love to have been there for that.

"Sam is taking him to try out adaptive equipment for a car. He's going to teach Mr. Cole to drive."

Carly choked. "Is that a good idea with the drinking?"

"Oh." The word came out as though she'd forgotten something important. "He hasn't had a drink since you left. He even gave Joe the bottles he was hiding."

Every last muscle in Carly's body released at those words. Praise God!

"Should I leave a message for him to call you?"

Her chest constricted. What would she say to him? Somehow begging him to continue therapy with her didn't seem appropriate, and she had no other reason to come back. "No, Mrs. Rivera. I just wanted to see how things were going. It appears he's doing well." *Without me.*

Carly pushed *end* on her cell, a loss hanging in the air. She headed down the stairs to where her father waited to have dinner. He mentioned he had something important to tell her and she shouldn't be late.

He put a large bowl on the dining-room table as she entered. "Finally. That phone call took a while."

She didn't tell him the extra time was spent in the mirror making sure her eyes didn't appear puffy and red.

"I've got good news—I think. I spoke with an acquaintance of mine this afternoon—an old competitor in the prosthetics business." He served out the spaghetti to her dish and smirked. "A man whose products always inspired me to improve mine."

Carly shook out the paper napkin, her mind wandering to the dinners she'd shared with Cole every evening. The already cut meat, the linen napkins, and the man in his crisply ironed slacks and dress shirt, with a droll expression ready to provoke her. Her ire had seemed to give him much pleasure given the crooked smile and spark of the eye it elicited.

She missed that.

"Carly."

Jolting back to the present, she met her father's gaze.

Dad tilted his head. "This is important. Listen."

"Of course."

"Corbin wants you to work for him." He sighed.

"What?"

"I know taking this position isn't the same as owning your own company—"

"Dad—"

"But this way you could provide more equipment to more amputees within—"

"Dad."

He stopped.

"I don't want to own my own company."

His mouth dropped open.

"I never wanted to work the business side." Carly pulled in oxygen for resolve. "All I've ever wanted was to provide the best product for each individual who needs it."

Dad's shock softened into a warm smile.

"Like my Dad." She smiled back. "I want to work with the amputees, listen to them and design products that will help. No sales. No fundraising. No investors."

"Then why did you agree to work with Mr. Harrison?"

She grimaced. "I wanted to help you regain your reputation back. I thought a new family company would do that."

Dad's brow creased. "It was never about my reputation, Carly. It's always been about the people. You working for Corbin gives you the opportunity to do that. I guess this is the best solution after all. He loves your socket design, and I know he'll make it a quality product. He can't wait to bring you on board."

She thought about the man who'd offered them so much. "But what about Cole?"

"If you really don't want to start a new company, we won't need his investment after all."

"But—"

"It seems you've wasted time with him. I'm sorry I didn't speak to Corbin sooner. I should have seen your heart. But at least now you have better choices."

And no reason to go back. She worked her face into a smile she didn't feel. Working for her father's friend was perfect—for her career. But how would she tell Cole this news? *I don't need you anymore.* Somehow that felt like a lie?

"I kissed him."

Her father's eyes shot wide at the whispered words. "Did he—?"

"No, Dad. *I* kissed *him*."

He searched her expression. "Do you love him?"

She stirred the spaghetti over and over until it looked like a hurricane in her plate. "I don't know, Dad. He confuses me. I think I'm falling for parts of him. But if he doesn't accept the help he needs, he will destroy everyone around him. That's not a way to begin a relationship."

Dad's nod was solemn as he took long moments, his gaze running over her expression. "Does he love you?"

Carly shrugged. "I think he's very grateful for what I've done for him." She shook her head. "I'm not sure he knows what love is."

Dad's stern features melted into something warm. "I sensed something about him those many months ago." His eyes took on a melancholy. "You know he never wanted to wear prosthetics again."

Carly nodded.

"He saved my life that night." He peeked up as if to check her thoughts. "I'm not talking about the accident."

"I know, Dad."

A small smile grew on Dad's face as he touched Carly's cheek. "Of course, you know. You are my discerning child." He blinked. "I suspect you see something special in him, too."

"I do." She swallowed. "But he's so bitter toward God."

"Then maybe it's best you're here ... for now. But be ready if God calls you back."

If?

His lips pulled up. "And don't forget, earnest prayer is mightier than anything you can do on your own." He released a breath. "And sometimes all we have."

~*~

Counseling always left Cole raw. Like he'd just opened old wounds and rubbed sand into them. And yet the sand seemed more an abrasive cleanser removing the infection that festered there. Still, as he returned home from the intensive session, he needed something to clot the blood.

Beckett's book.

Cole's counselor told him group therapy would be helpful. He said there were many others who've come back from war with the same dreams, same flashbacks, same guilt. Did others have Becketts in their lives who'd fallen on IEDs for them? Cole wanted to know.

A group was out of the question in the remote town of Fairwilde. Not a haven for vets, so there weren't enough people to populate a gathering of that nature.

But could Fairwilde be a haven? A safe place. A retreat.

Cole shook his head. Who cared enough to make such a place happen?

Carly would. She was just the type. Always wanting to help others, especially veterans. But Cole had also done some research on substance abuse and the people who loved those who suffered from it. He wondered if his need was the only thing that drew Carly to him. What did they call it? Codependency. Not a healthy basis for a relationship. He wanted her to love him for him.

Like he loved her.

Oh, those words left a chasm in his chest.

He needed to get whole before he invited her back in his life—if he ever did. Would she want him?

He tromped down the hall to his bedroom and found the Bible on his nightstand. He'd read about Jesus over the past few weeks and found Him not quite the taskmaster he'd envisioned Him to be. He was more the wise counselor. Gentle king. So righteous and yet forgiving. Cole would love to meet someone like that.

Meet me.

Cole no longer flinched at the words that sounded in his soul. They'd become more commonplace as he read of the God of the Bible. "Speak to me, Lord."

No more words came. Only the feeling the book he held needed to be opened. He'd already read all the Gospels. He flipped the pages to get to the next book, Beckett's notecards stopping him in places here and there. He would read every one of those cards one day, but only as he came to the passages they'd referred to in the Bible. Flipping some more, the pages halted at an envelope. The words on the front of it captured him: Second Lieutenant Cole Harrison.

Cole pulled it out. What could it be? He'd already read the note from Beckett's mother weeks ago. Was this from his dad? Maybe—if Beckett inherited his awful script from his father.

Cole's tongue itched for the burn of a good drink. Could he bear another missive from a member of the Forsythe household? He almost dropped to the floor to scavenge under his bed for a bag that might not have been removed, but he knew Joe had emptied every last one.

Curse it!

Cole's hands shook as he inserted his index finger into the gap of the envelope and tore the top.

He grasped the bottom with a light grip of the prosthesis—a grip he'd practiced with Sam over the past several weeks—and tugged the page carefully so as not to endanger it. Something told him he couldn't lose these words.

He drew in a breath. Without the alcohol he'd need something stronger to sustain him. He looked to the ceiling. "Help me, Lord. I don't think I can do this."

You can't ... without me.

"Yes, God." The words escaped in such a whisper Cole wasn't sure he'd said them out loud.

His hand shook as he unfolded the page. The muscles in his face twinged as the handwriting confirmed Cole's deepest fears. He read:

Dear Sir,

You may laugh at this crazy message, given right now I'm perfectly healthy. But then again, if you are holding this letter it means the thing I believe is going to happen ... well ... did.

I'm writing you because I had a dream last night—a scary and wonderful dream. I know you don't believe in Jesus and all that, but He came to me in a vision. You may say He was a figment of my imagination, but I could feel the warmth of the light emanating from his body and smell the wood on Him from his carpentry work. I've never had a dream like that before. It was somehow more real than being awake.

Jesus said He'd be taking me home tomorrow. I flinched at the vision of how that would occur, but he laid His pierced hand on my shoulder and told me, "Do not be afraid." Suddenly, I wasn't. Love and security washed over me like I'd never known.

I wondered if I'd miss my family, and He told me they'd be with me before I noticed they weren't. I didn't know if that meant they'd also die soon or that I'd be too busy in heaven to think of them much. Funny the weird things that came to mind in the presence of my Savior.

Jesus told me what I was going to do tomorrow would take an instant, but its effects would last generations. Those words comforted me because it has always been my goal to honor Him with my life. He told me it would honor Him, and gave me a vision of what that meant for you. I can't tell you the awe I felt at seeing who you will become. It makes the sacrifice more than worth it.

Please know, sir, I am ready to go home to be with the Lord today. My only regret is that I couldn't live longer to do more for my God, but He assures me I have done all He requires. I am at peace.

It's funny. I feel stupid writing these things right now. What if my dream is just a dream and I rip these pages tomorrow night because the vision was untrue. Still, it feels good to at least have the courage to tell you about my God and Savior, even if you only see this after I'm gone. I've always been scared to evangelize. Guess I'm not too brave. But sometimes a man needs to speak. If not through his words, through his actions.

Cole (I use your given name now because Jesus tells me you are my brother), I look forward to the time I will see you again.

Beckett Forsythe

Courage?! The page shook in Cole's hand. He couldn't believe the man who fell on an IED felt he lacked courage. Cole pulled his sleeve across his face to dry the tears, sniffed back the gunk that gathered in his throat, and stood. He needed to pace.

What did he mean about the awe he'd felt in seeing the man Cole would become? This useless wretch who wore his bitterness like a rotten soup stain. He sat on the bed and peered into the opened Bible, at the page where Beckett's letter had been hidden. Had Beckett's parents seen this or did they, as did Cole, assume it was another index card of notes?

The printed words in the book became a jumble through the tears that refused to end ... until his gaze fell on the familiar verse.

While we were still sinners, Christ died for us.

Those were the words Carly had spoken to him. Beckett had died for Cole, knowing Cole was a drunk. Knowing he'd been unworthy to lead his men that day. And yet, Beckett risked it all so Cole could live. What had he known?

What had this Jesus told him?

Cole rummaged through his closet to find his suitcase. Bits of manila envelope from the package still littered the floor inside. *Thank you.* He mouthed the words to his Creator as he found the pieces fit together just enough to show the return address of Mr. and Mrs. Forsythe. They hadn't been thrown away like the rest of the envelope.

He tromped to the chest-of-drawers and drew out pajamas, socks, shirts, etc. Everything he'd need for a trip. Manny could take him to the airport. Hopefully there was a flight out by tomorrow. Otherwise he'd chicken out before he got there. He needed to talk to Beckett's parents. He needed to tell them the truth about himself and what Beckett had done for him.

He also wanted to know if Beckett had told them of his dream or what Jesus said about who Cole would become. Because Cole had no clue. He wanted to be something worthy of Beckett's act, but he couldn't fathom it—an impossibility.

Nothing is impossible with Me.

The image of Mrs. Forsythe spitting in his face when she discovered who Cole really was played relentlessly through his mind. Cole hadn't helped her son. Still, he knew she had the answer he was looking for. And he was willing to bear her contempt to find it.

Chapter Seventeen

"Hi, Joe, it's me." Carly was so glad to hear his voice. It had been an intense few months dealing with her brothers' lawsuit and her father's feelings of guilt. Still, the dropping of the criminal charges had eased her mind.

"Carly, so good to hear you. I've been watching the news about the trial. So sorry to hear the company is going out of business."

Carly warmed at his concern. "It's okay, Joe. What the company had become was no longer my father's dream. God has given us other opportunities to help vets." She'd spoken to her father's friend and they'd already begun to develop some of her designs.

"Glad to hear that." Carly loved the smile in Joe's voice.

"So how's Cole doing?" A part of her hoped he'd slowed his progress, a reason for her to return.

"He's doing well." Joe's tone was guarded. What was he hiding? "He even went on a trip last week."

"A trip?" That didn't sound like the recluse she'd come to know. "Where'd he go?"

"I don't know. He wouldn't tell us."

She sensed a hesitation. "What are you leaving out, Joe?"

His breath blew against the receiver. "It's just that he came back very intense and has been having lunch with Charles Jurvis every day since."

Carly's shoulders sunk. "That's the man who brought him the alcohol, isn't it?"

"Yes."

"Is he coming home drunk?"

"I can't tell. But sometimes alcoholics are good at hiding it, especially when those around them are used to the behavior."

"Joe, you'd know." She was certain of that.

He sighed. "I thought I would, but he's been so quiet and to himself, I don't know what to make of him."

"When I come, we'll pray together."

A horse whinnied in the background.

"Joe? What are you not saying?"

"Cole isn't getting regular physical therapy anymore. Only check-ups now and then."

She swallowed the lump in her throat. "Oh, um, I guess I'm not needed."

"Carly—"

"That's okay, Joe. I understand. That's good news." And somehow not. "Did you tell him about my job?" She'd hoped Joe could break it to him better than she could.

"How you won't need his investment?"

Why did that sound so awful? "Yes."

"I told him."

"What did he say?" What had she hoped he'd say?

"He said he was glad for you."

That was all?

"Carly, you can come to visit us?"

She shook her head. "I really shouldn't right now. If Cole no longer needs me for therapy, I should focus on my new job."

"You don't have to be needed to come here. Just because people don't need each other, doesn't mean they don't want each other."

Carly flinched at the words. Did she want Cole? She knew the answer to that question, but wasn't ready to admit it to Joe. It'd be like serving her heart up to be sliced. Cole didn't want her. He'd only been grateful for how she'd helped him. Now that his therapy was complete, he probably didn't even think of her—except to erase all the messages she'd left ... messages he'd never returned. "I can't Joe. Not now." She fiddled with the cross at her neck. "But please call again and let me know how everyone is doing."

"Sure."

Chapter Eighteen

The beauty of the fall colors astounded Carly as she drove up the forested road. How could Cole not believe in God when surrounded by such an extraordinary array?

What would she find when she got to the manor? Why had Joe made her promise to come? Her mind played back the conversation she'd had with him weeks ago and how he suspected Cole had been drinking again. Could Joe need her to challenge him? Was she stepping into an intervention?

It had been many months since she'd lived at the Harrison mansion. She missed every one of its occupants. Her heart ached at the thought of seeing them again, as she anticipated the pain of leaving already.

Carly turned into the tree-lined drive. It was like threading through a multi-colored tunnel. Reds and yellows swathed the green overhead, with more gold, red and brown from the fallen leaves below. Magical.

Enchanted.

The drive opened to the manor. Usually empty pavement, but today it was alive with activity. Trucks with ladders, vans of tradesman and building supplies all scattered around with men in coveralls coming in and out as though the manor were receiving an overhaul.

Mrs. Rivera opened the door to one of the men, giving him a sour face as she pointed to a side entrance. He pivoted and followed her direction. Her head shook as she wiped her hands on the apron around her waist.

Carly just wanted to hug the woman.

In fact, she'd do that right now.

Mrs. Rivera almost closed the door before she saw her. Her eyes lit and she strode to envelop Carly to her bosom. "My dear, you have been gone too long." She eyed her up and down. "You're too skeeny. We fatten you up tonight."

Carly chuckled. "I didn't come for dinner."

"Nonsense. You stay."

"I came because Joe wanted to see me."

"See you?" Mrs. Rivera smiled and held out her hands. "Or have you see this?"

Carly's gaze followed the gesture. "What's going on here anyway?"

Mrs. Rivera's brown eyes glinted as she wrapped an arm around Carly and pulled her inside. "You come."

Carly could barely hear with all the noise—circular saws, drills, hammering, and who-knows-what. A huge hole, the size of a large closet, lay open in the wall by the stairs.

"He installs an elevator." Mrs. Rivera explained with pride in her accented voice.

"But he can use the stairs with the prosthesis Why an elevator now?"

"This is not for him. It is for his guests."

Carly thought of the parties that once filled these halls and imagined drunken models in sequined gowns. An emptiness burned through her. Would

Cole go back to the life his parents had lived now that she'd provided him with limbs? How could Mrs. Rivera see that as a good thing? Carly wanted to shake him.

"You are not pleased?" The Mexican accent intensified with the bunching of Mrs. Rivera's brows.

What could Carly say?

"Many vets will be healed here."

"Vets?"

"Jes. Did Joe not tell you? Cole is turning us into a retreat center."

Carly laughed at the way it sounded, as though Mrs. Rivera would transform with an enchantment on the manor. "A retreat center?" Too many questions running through her head to even begin to ask.

Mrs. Rivera pointed to the hole in the wall. "The elevator will take them to their suites. They will receive state-of-the-art prosthetics. From the company you work for, no doubt." She winked. "They will receive physical therapy, psychotherapy and … what is it Sam calls his horse stuff?"

Horse stuff?

"Hippotherapy."

"Jes, hippy-therapy." Mrs. Rivera ignored Carly's giggle. "Mr. Cole plans to take them on trails in the woods. He says many vets feel more comfortable in the elements. They will go camping." She shuddered. "Eat squirrel probably."

The back door slid open. Joe stepped inside. "Carly, you came."

Carly swallowed the lump in her throat. She'd missed them all more than she'd known. Her eyes burned. "Where's Cole?"

"And hello to you too." Joe's eyes lit with mock insult.

She hugged him. "It's so good to see you. I'm just so amazed at what's happening here. And ..."

"You want to ask him about it."

"Yes, of course, Joe." She sobered thinking of the last conversation they'd had about Cole. "Is he drinking?"

Joe shook his head. "Wait till you see him." His smile broadened.

"What do you mean?" She took in the looks Mrs. Rivera and Joe shared, but they said nothing.

Joe pushed her out the back door. "He's at his favorite place. You know where that is. Go find him."

~*~

Would she remember the trail Cole took her through so long ago? She'd walked it many times herself, mesmerized at how God had repurposed the marred tree from her father's accident. New growth in broken spots and animals finding shelter in the holes. What would it look like now in all its autumn glory?

The leaves rustled at her feet as she turned right at the fork in the path. The crisp air cooled the skin on her cheeks. She spied the rooted incline ahead. Her pulse raced in her ears and made her dizzy. What would she say to this man she'd grown to love? Could she tell him how she felt? Would he laugh at her now that he no longer needed her?

The scent of fall filled her nose and lungs as she took in its sustenance and set her foot on the first divot to climb. Pulling herself up using all fours, she reached the top and startled.

A stranger sat at the edge, looking over the forest below. He turned at her gasp. "Carly?"

Could that be Cole's voice coming from the person with thick, wavy brown hair? He turned, the scar coming into view and she almost cried at the beauty of the man. "Cole?"

He stood and strode to her, pulling her to her feet. The eyes that no longer held dark circles, took her in with consternation. "What are you doing here?"

"Joe asked me to come." Now she felt stupid. Like an interloper. She didn't belong here.

He stood as though a wall held him from her.

~*~

Her presence had shaken Cole. He'd thought he could bear Carly's lack in his life, but looking at her now, he knew that was not true. "Why did Joe ask you here?"

Or the better question, why did he bother to orchestrate something that couldn't be. She'd been hesitant toward his advances in the beginning and found the first opportunity to leave when she had the chance. He didn't want her kisses, knowing she'd only given them out of pity.

Her face pinched as she shook her head, uncertainty filling her expression. "I guess he wanted to show me your retreat." The smile that flickered on her lips gave him hope that she was pleased. Her eyes drifted to the edge of his perch. She squinted. "Is that a Bible?"

He pulled her to the spot where he now looked upon God's glory in radiant fall colors, and gestured for her to sit with him. "It's Beckett's Bible."

"Beckett's Bible?" Her eyes searched his soul.

He smiled at the incredulity in her tone and drew in a breath. "Sent from the grave."

Her mouth hung open.

"He'd asked his parents to send it to me if something happened to him. They only got around to it a few months ago."

She still didn't speak.

"Inside was a letter from Beckett. He'd had a premonition he'd die to save me and wanted to explain."

"A premonition?" The brown in Carly's eyes grew deeper as tears filled them. He wanted to know every level of their depth—even if he drowned there.

"I went to see his parents a while back to tell them of their son's bravery. I expected them to hate me for my role in his death." A lump formed in his gut. He sniffed. "His mother thanked me for sharing such good news."

Carly tilted her head. He loved the way she didn't speak when she knew he needed time to process his thoughts.

"Good news," he repeated, still not believing the woman's words. "In fact, she apologized for not getting the Bible to me sooner. She said because of her, my healing had been delayed." He closed his eyes at the image of the woman sobbing at what she had called her own selfishness.

"What's happening to you?" Carly's gaze seemed to search every angle of his face.

He took her hand in his intact one. "I'm becoming whole." His thumb traveled her palm. "I think the Bible would call it, a new creation."

A tear rolled down her cheek. Cole wanted to stop it with his lips.

"You believe?" So much riding on her voice in that question. How much did she want that for him? Why did she want that for him?

He nodded.

Her hand encircled his. It felt so right. "Mrs. Rivera told me you were preparing for guests and I worried you were going back to a partying life."

"I am." His lips curled in spite of himself. "At least one more. It was Jurvis's idea."

She grimaced. "Why does that worry me?"

"You see, The David Project—that's what I plan to call this retreat—"

"The David Project?"

"I wanted to call it the Beckett Forsythe Memorial Veteran's Retreat, but Beckett's family assured me he'd have hated that. They said he wouldn't want attention to be drawn to him, only to his Savior." Cole squeezed Carly's fingers. "That sounded just like Beckett, so I decided to name it after his favorite person in the Bible—other than Jesus, of course. The one who inspired Beckett to be a warrior for God. The man who was able to put his service in perspective because he honored and trusted his Creator."

"I like that." She peered out over the forest of colors, her gaze seeming to rest on the tree her father had hit. "So what about this party?"

"Well, I may be made of money, but it will take additional funds to keep a retreat like this going long term. So I asked Jurvis to help me. He drummed up some of my parent's influential contacts and devised a fundraising gala to bring awareness to it. We'll be hosting guests all next weekend."

"That's wonderful." Carly stood, her voice flat. "It appears you have it all worked out." Was she going to leave him there?

Cole lifted from the grass and brushed the leaves off his jeans. He couldn't let her go. He needed to do something to keep her there.

God, you've been with me through all the risks I've taken these last few months. Be with me now.

"Since you're here, there's something I'd like to know." He closed in on Carly and traced a wayward strand of blond from her eyes. The scent of her coconut lotion filled him with the confidence to ask. "Will you be my date for the gala?" There was so much more he wanted to say, but he didn't want to scare her.

Her gaze lifted to his, wonder or amazement streaming through it. Her lips parted. What would her answer be?

He swallowed hard. "Well?"

She seemed to scan his hairline, his face, questions in her eyes. "You want me to be your date?"

"And so much more," he said on a breath, pulling her to his chest, her heart beating in tandem with his. "Will you?"

She rested her head on his shirt. "Yes, I will."

Cole smoothed her hair with his hand as a familiar image infiltrated his thoughts. "Just make sure you wear a yellow ball gown." A chuckle rumbled within. "You know, the kind with puffy sleeves and a big hoop skirt."

She pulled from him and raised a brow. "I don't do hoops."

"If you don't have one, I'll buy it for you." He tried an innocent look.

She scowled. "And you can nix the puffy sleeves idea, too."

He blinked. "You'd begrudge a man his fantasy." His lips tugged up against his will.

"I'll give you the yellow part."

His gaze scanned her mud-smudged jeans. "Fine, wear something slinky and skin-tight if you must. Just no dirty denim at my gala." He couldn't resist. "And no changing tires beforehand either."

Her hand came up to touch the scar at his lip with her thumb. Her fingers so soft. Her voice a whisper. "Now there's the man I know and lo—"

He kissed her forehead. "Ha! I caught that. You love me." The grin was relentless now.

She twisted her lips. "Don't let it go to your head."

He squeezed her tighter. She felt so good in his arms—the one arm given from God, the other from Carly. Fitting. Those he loved most. "That's okay. The feeling is very mutual."

Author Note

Thank you for reading *At the Edge of a Dark Forest*. If you enjoyed it please take a moment to write a review at your favorite retailer.

Visit me at LivingtheBodyofChrist.blogspot.com OR InfiniteCharacters.com

Follow me on Twitter, Facebook and Pinterest. See you on the web!

Thank you!

Connie Almony

Acknowledgements:

As we often say in the writing biz, books do not happen in a vacuum. They require help and sacrifice from the people around them. The first to sacrifice was my husband, who, when I said I wanted to write a novel, replied, "Okay, I'll do the laundry." Wow! I did not expect that. Thank you, dear! In that vein, I should also thank my children, who have to bear with my husband's idea of laundry and my frequent response to their questions that goes something like this, "Don't talk to me now, I'm in story world." You guys have been extraordinarily patient with me. Don't think I haven't noticed.

Thank you to my critique partners who virtually taught me how to write: June Foster, Gail Palotta, Vanessa Riley, and Mildred Colvin. Their fairytale retellings (the rest of the Fairwilde Reflections) are mentioned at the back of this book. Though Jean Huffman is not an official critique partner, she was good enough to help me with the final polish. Thank you, sistah.

So I didn't make up any new laws that might get me into trouble, I consulted my Gomer (Third-Day-Psycho-Fan) buddy, Breauna Murphy on the legal stuff.

ACKNOWLEDGEMENTS

Thank you beta readers, Jan Wisooker and Jody Kilmer.

A couple years before this project was conceptualized, I did a Military ministries series on my blog LivingtheBodyofChrist.Blogspot.com. I came across a real, Christ-centered ministry for the military and their families now called CruMilitary and received lots of suggestions from Jean King. I was very impressed with the resources they provide churches to help our veterans and therefore have chosen to donate 10% of my earnings on this novella to their ministry. I hope you will check out their website and consider using their resources to start a ministry of your own.

A book cannot be written without inspiration. I received it from many sources, all at the Holy Spirit's leading—Thank you God. I want to thank our members of the military and their families for all they do to keep us safe and free. Thank you NEEDTOBREATHE for being the muse on this one. You always help me delve into the emotional depths of the characters and the hard roads they travel.

Lastly, I want to thank Julie and Randall Alley for allowing me to use Randall's High Fidelity Interface Socket design in the story. Julie was so good to share with me about the field of prosthetic creation. Any mistakes or inaccuracies in this work are solely mine. If you'd like to find out more about the High Fidelity Socket, check out their website http://www.biodesigns.com/. It's really cool!!!

Reading Group Questions

1. At the Edge of a Dark Forest is a modern-day re-telling of Beauty and the Beast. In what ways did this story depart from the original? Do you feel it detracted or enhanced the re-telling?
2. Cole feels his disfigurement is just punishment for the self-absorbed man he'd been. Do you have events in your own life that you carry as a form of punishment, not accepting the grace Jesus has given you?
3. Cole is not very nice to Carly when she first arrives, but she eventually sees there is more to him than his gruff exterior. What is the best way to approach someone like Cole?
4. Carly is gifted at listening to her clients and providing products that will meet their needs. She almost gave up using that gift to fulfill what she thought were her father's dreams. Have you given up what you know is God's calling in order to pursue things others have told you to do?
5. When Cole first sees Carly, he notices she is very plain. He calls her "Beauty" to mock her, but eventually the mocking turns into a term of endearment. What do you think he is responding to?

6. Carly explains to Cole what it means for a person to "slay a dragon" for another—to take a personal risk to give that person something he or she needs. What dragons have been slayed for you by those who love you? Have you shown your appreciation to them for doing so?
7. As things seem to be crumbling in Cole's life, Carly is called away. What do you think God was doing in Cole's life at that time, and do you think Carly responded appropriately?
8. Beckett's favorite book of the Bible is Psalms because most of them were written by whom he called "A Warrior King." Beckett related both to the author's profession as well as his heart for God. Though Cole finds peace in many of those verses, he is most touched by a verse in the letters of Paul. What is the book of the Bible you most relate to today, and which did you relate most to when you first became a Christian?
9. God placed many good people in Cole's life—those who led him, counseled him, cared for him and challenged him. Do you have people who do these things for you? In what ways?
10. Eventually, God used Cole's ugliness, brokenness and emptiness to help others suffering from the effects of war. How has God used negative events in your life for His glory?
11. At one point, Carly had to decide between staying with Cole as he spiraled downward, and helping her father. Joe tells her God is calling her away so He can do the work with

Cole alone. Have you ever had to "let go" of someone you cared for so God could work in his or her life?

About the Author

Connie's experience includes working as a Christian Counselor in Columbia, Maryland. Though she no longer counsels, she continues to work with wonderful people in this field. She has been married over twenty years to a man who graciously encourages her new writing obsession, and has two beautiful children who inspire her to become all she can be.

Connie hosts the blog LivingtheBodyofChrist.Blogspot.com created to encourage readers to use their God-given gifts. She also writes for InfiniteCharacters.com, a group blog dedicated to guide writers in their pursuit of a dream, and readers in their pursuit of a good read.

Follow her on Twitter, Facebook, Goodreads and Pinterest.

Coming Soon, More Fairwilde Reflections …

Red and the Wolf, by June Foster—April 2014
Newspaper reporter Lilly *Red* Hood forgot her dinner date with Handsome Hunter Woods, thanks to ADD she's had since childhood. In Hunter's absence, fellow reporter Wolf Skinner moves in with less than honorable intentions. When Lilly gets lost in the Alabama forest, which of these men will be her hero?

Mirror Mirror, by Mildred Colvin—June 2014
Can anything else go wrong? Sonya White's beloved stepmother has cancer, she is told Eric Price, the man she loves is after her family's money, then it appears someone wants her dead. She runs—right into the enemy's clutches.

Mountain of Love and Danger, by Gail Palotta—July 2014
Jack Greenthumb's having fun—a different day—a different girl. Then his dad's farm's destroyed; the girl he really loves, kidnapped. Thrust into manhood and bravery, Jack spies on criminals, scales a treacherous mountain and confronts a giant to set things right before everything's ruined.

AND …

Swept Away, by Vanessa Riley—August 2014
Charlotte Downing, the Duchess of Charming, wants what she wants. Today, it's a fine pair of lacy slippers crafted by the renowned Ella's Establishment, but the conservative proprietor, Edwin Cinder, has rejected her offer. When a London gale crashes ceilings and traps the two, will hearts change and opposites work together for survival?

Find out more at InfiniteCharacters.com/fairwilde-reflections/

Made in the USA
Lexington, KY
20 January 2017